PUFFIN BOOKS

The Bomber Dog

Megan Rix lives with her husband by a river in England. When she's not writing she can be found walking her two golden retrievers, Traffy and Bella, who are often in the river.

Books by Megan Rix

The Bomber Dog

megan rix

PUFFIN

PUFFIN BOOKS

Published by the Penguin Group
Penguin Books Ltd, 80 Strand, London WC2R 0RL, England
Penguin Group (USA) Inc., 375 Hudson Street, New York, New York 10014, USA
Penguin Group (Canada), 90 Eglinton Avenue East, Suite 700, Toronto, Ontario, Canada M4P 2Y3
(a division of Pearson Penguin Canada Inc.)
Penguin Ireland, 25 St Stephen's Green, Dublin 2, Ireland (a division of Penguin Books Ltd)
Penguin Group (Australia), 707 Collins Street, Melbourne, Victoria 3008, Australia
(a division of Pearson Australia Group Pty Ltd)
Penguin Books India Pvt Ltd, 11 Community Centre, Panchsheel Park, New Delhi – 110 017, India
Penguin Group (NZ), 67 Apollo Drive, Rosedale, Auckland 0632, New Zealand
(a division of Pearson New Zealand Ltd)
Penguin Books (South Africa) (Pty) Ltd, Block D, Rosebank Office Park, 181 Jan Smuts Avenue,
Parktown North, Gauteng 2193, South Africa

Penguin Books Ltd, Registered Offices: 80 Strand, London WC2R 0RL, England

puffinbooks.com

First published 2013
001

Text copyright © Megan Rix, 2013
Map and illustrations copyright © Puffin Books, 2013
Map by David Atkinson
Illustrations by Sara Chadwick-Holmes
All rights reserved

Set in 13/20 pt Baskerville MT
Typeset by Palimpsest Book Production Ltd, Falkirk, Stirlingshire
Printed in Great Britain by Clays Ltd, St Ives plc

British Library Cataloguing in Publication Data
A CIP catalogue record for this book is available from the British Library

ISBN: 978-0-141-34789-9

www.greenpenguin.co.uk

ALWAYS LEARNING   **PEARSON**

'For Gallantry, We Also Serve'

Prologue

Occupied France, 1940

Sabine knew what the soldiers had come for as soon as she saw them marching down the muddy lane to their farmhouse. Her hands shook as she grabbed the nearest of the twelve-week-old German Shepherd puppies and ran out of the wooden back door with it.

Her younger brother, Claude, was outside feeding the chickens.

'What is it? What's going on? Where are you taking that puppy?' he called out.

The German soldiers were almost at the farmhouse. There wasn't time for Sabine to explain.

'Tell the soldiers one of the puppies died,' she said. 'Do you understand? Tell them he was the smallest and weakest of the litter and he wasn't strong enough to survive and he died.'

Claude's blue eyes opened very wide. 'But that's not true,' he said.

'Just say it!' Sabine shouted.

The puppy, frightened by the harshness of her voice, wriggled to get away but she clung on to him.

'You're not going to kill it, are you?' Claude said, his eyes filling with tears. 'You wouldn't . . . You couldn't.'

Those tears would help convince the soldiers that what he said was true.

The Germans were now so close she could hear their voices as they entered the farmhouse. She heard her mother screaming at them not to take the puppies away. Alsatians, or German Shepherd Wolf Dogs, as they were also known, were highly prized by the Nazis. They were famed for their intelligence, strength and bravery, making them ideal dogs to train up for war duty. Herr Hitler owned two of them.

'No,' Sabine told her brother. 'It's a lie. Just tell them what I told you. At least this one will be safe.'

Claude nodded once, dropped his pot of corn on the ground, and ran back to the farmhouse. The chickens clucked with excitement as they rushed to peck at their unexpected feast.

Sabine looked behind her and then ran the other way. It wasn't easy to run with a wriggling, heavy, furry bundle in her arms, but if she could save just one of the pups from becoming part of the war, it would be worth it.

The puppy was still very young and not used to being snatched away from his mother or being squeezed so tightly, but there wasn't time to stop and reassure him.

Sabine ran so hard it felt like her heart was beating almost out of her chest and her breathing came in painful gasps, but she wouldn't stop. Not even when she got a stitch in her side. She couldn't stop. She had to save the puppy.

The British undercover soldiers were boarding the rowing boat hidden by the newly formed French Resistance as she ran up to them.

'Please take this puppy with you. Please save him,' she begged.

Ever since France had been occupied by Germany, a few brave fighters had formed a group known as the Resistance. It was a secret organization made up of ordinary French people and their aim was to do anything they could to undermine the German occupation of their country. They were being helped by

British soldiers from across the English Channel, but their work was incredibly dangerous and secretive. Sabine's father was part of the French Resistance, just as her brother and mother were.

The Resistance had started with just a few people, but it had gradually grown and grown. Not everyone was a member though, and Sabine and Claude's mother always warned them that they had to be very careful who they told.

'Whatever happens, the flame of the French resistance must not be extinguished and will not be extinguished,' General de Gaulle had said in a broadcast on the radio.

But he was now in London and they were on the front line in France.

There were rumours that if the German army found out they were part of the Resistance they would be taken away and put in a prisoner-of-war camp.

Chapter 1

Close to the white cliffs of Dover, a little German Shepherd puppy cowered away from the seagulls that circled menacingly above him. He'd tried to run away from the birds but they were bigger and faster than he was. He'd barked at them but the seagulls' cries only seemed to mock his high puppy yap.

Molly, a honey-coated spaniel, spotted the puppy and the gulls near the docks. She barked and ran at the large, sharp-beaked birds, scattering them into the drizzly sky of the early February morning. The gulls dodged the silver barrage balloons that floated high in the air, and circled to land on the warships anchored in the harbour, screeching in protest. But they didn't return.

Once they'd gone, the rain-soaked, floppy-eared, sable-coated puppy came over to his rescuer, whimpering and trembling with fear and cold. Molly licked his blue-eyed face to reassure him and he nuzzled into her. His pitiful cries were gradually calming but his desperate hunger remained.

Molly used her nose to knock over a glass bottle of milk that the milkman had just left at the Dover harbour master's door. The bottle smashed and the puppy's little pink tongue lapped thirstily at the milk that flowed on to the ground.

'Get away from that!' the milkman yelled angrily, when he saw the puppy drinking. His boot kicked out at him, only narrowly missing the puppy's little legs. Molly barked at the milkman and she and the pup ran off together with the milkman's furious shouts still ringing in their ears.

The smell of the sea and the reek of the oil from the ships grew fainter as they ran, but the small dog wasn't strong enough to run for very long yet, and they slowed to a walk as soon as they left the docks. Molly led the puppy through the outskirts of Dover to her den, a derelict garden shed at the edge of the allotments. There was sacking on the floor, it had a solid waterproof roof, and as an added bonus, every now and again a foolish rat or mouse would enter the shed – only to be pounced on and eagerly gulped down.

The tired puppy sank down on the sacking and immediately fell fast asleep, exhausted from the morning's excitement. Britain was in the grip of the Second World War, and Dover was a crucially important port, constantly filled with the hustle and bustle of ships and soldiers, but the puppy was blissfully unaware of all that.

Molly lay down too, her head resting on her paws, but she didn't sleep; she watched over her new companion.

Only a few weeks ago, Molly had been a much-loved pet, until a bomb had hit the house she lived in.

She remembered her owner being put on a stretcher and rushed to hospital, but Molly herself hadn't been found. She'd stayed hidden amid the rubble, shaking uncontrollably, too traumatized to make a sound.

She'd stayed in exactly the same spot for the rest of the night, covered in debris, too scared to sleep. At dawn she'd crawled out of her hiding place and taken her first tentative steps towards the shattered window and the world outside, alone.

The puppy snuffled in his sleep and Molly licked him gently until he settled. There were hundreds, maybe thousands, of lost and abandoned dogs in Dover but at least she and this baby Alsatian had found each other.

For the first few weeks, the puppy stayed as close to Molly as he could, never allowing the two of them to get more than a few steps apart. Wherever she went he followed her, not wanting to be left alone again, even for a moment.

Every night they lay close together on the sacking and kept each other warm, listening to the bomber planes as they flew overhead on their way to London and other cities.

As the weeks turned into months, and winter turned into spring and then summer, the bomber planes and the bombs they dropped became so commonplace that they no longer woke Molly or her young friend, curled up together in the shed.

Now one year old, the German Shepherd

was no longer the vulnerable puppy he'd once been, but Molly still licked his furry sable head to soothe him when he twitched and cried out in his sleep. He still had the same piercing blue eyes he'd had as a young puppy, but one of his ears now stood straight up, while the other still flopped down. With Molly's care and love he'd grown fast and he was now much larger and stronger than her, but she was still definitely the leader of their two-dog pack.

Their first priority each day was always to find food – and the most delicious food in the world, just waiting for a dog to help himself, was in the pig bins.

Two or more tin dustbins were set on most street corners for people's waste food. These dustbins were collected every week and taken out to farms to feed the pigs. Although the bins were emptied regularly, they still attracted flies, especially in the warm summer weather.

Molly and the German Shepherd didn't

mind about the bluebottles that buzzed around the bins. In fact, the young dog sometimes forgot the reason they'd come to the pig bins in his excitement at trying to catch one. He'd jump and snap at the insects as they flew out of the pig bins and buzzed around him, almost taunting him, daring him to try and catch them. He did dare, but however hard he tried, he only occasionally managed to swallow one.

Molly would remind him with a look or a whine, and occasionally even a bark, that they were at the pig bins to eat. Then he would stick his head in the bin and gorge himself until he could eat no more. Sometimes the leftovers had only just been put in the bin and were fresh, but more often, if the bins hadn't been emptied in the previous few days, they were rancid and mouldy. The dogs ate them anyway, ate and ate and ate.

Today, Molly led her young friend to two

bins at the bottom of a dead-end street. He skilfully knocked the lid off the first one and then sneezed with excitement at the tantalizing smell coming from inside it. The next moment all that could be seen of him was a fiercely wagging tail as his sensitive nose investigated the intriguing scent coming from the bottom of the bin. He was so busy trying to reach it that he didn't even hear the growl.

But Molly did. She turned to find five vicious-looking feral dogs spoiling for a fight. The growl had come from their leader: a large rough-furred, yellow-toothed, muscular dog that towered menacingly over Molly.

Molly gave a low, warning growl in return.

It was at this moment that the German Shepherd emerged, triumphant, to show Molly what he'd found. The ham bone had been right at the bottom of the bin, and old potato peelings and cabbage leaves dropped from him as he rose. He hadn't expected to find five snarling dogs waiting for him. The brutish-looking leader drooled at the sight of the bone.

The dogs' faces twisted into snarls as they headed towards him. There was only one way out – he leapt from the pig bin and raced past them and out on to the main street. The feral dogs turned and charged after him, while Molly ran after them, barking loudly.

He raced down one street, and up another, and still they followed him. They were big dogs and looked better fed than him, but he was much quicker.

The large ham bone was heavy in his mouth and slippery in his jaws, but he wouldn't let it go, not even when one of the pack got so close he could hear it breathing. He doubled back through an alleyway, dodged left then twisted right, racing on through the graveyard, and back through a concealed hole in the fence and into the allotments, where he hid in the blackberry bushes. He panted as he listened intently for the sound of the other dogs, but there was nothing. He'd successfully lost them and he gnawed on his ham bone trophy with relish.

Molly found him a few minutes later and came up to him, out of breath. He dropped the bone and nudged it over to her with his nose. She wagged her tail in thanks and gnawed on it. The bone had been worth it and they took it in turns to chew on it until it was quite gone.

At twilight they made their way back to their den in the old disused shed.

The blackout had been in force since the beginning of the war, so with no street lights on and with clouds hiding the stars, it grew very dark very quickly.

Usually the young dog paid very little attention to the high wailing sound of the air-raid siren.

It was such a common noise, one he'd heard since he was born and he, like many other pets, knew instinctively when no bomber planes were headed in their direction and there was nothing to fear.

But tonight was different. Tonight the hackles along his back rose and he sat up and listened to the strange, almost bird-like whistling sound. Tonight he was afraid. He got to his feet but there wasn't time to run before the bomb fell. A deafening roar filled his ears and for a moment the whole world seemed to collapse around him. The force of the blast threw him across the shed, and he lay still as the dusty air swirled about him.

For a moment he was knocked out, but as soon as he came to, he belly-crawled over to Molly who lay unconscious on the ground.

He whined and nuzzled his head against hers but her eyes didn't open. He lay down beside her to keep her warm and listened as outside in the street people called to each other, fire-engine bells rang and ambulances screeched to a halt.

Then he smelt a new smell. The smell of smoke. A spark from the burning houses had fallen on the shed and now it began to smoulder.

The dog whined again and then barked at Molly, but still she didn't stir. He pawed at his friend, instinctively knowing that the smell meant serious danger.

In desperation he barked again and then he took hold of Molly's collar with his teeth and pulled. Although Molly was much smaller than he was it was still almost impossible for him to drag her leaden body across the uneven ground. He lost his grip, whined, then gripped her collar more firmly in his teeth and crouched low so he could pull her with every ounce of strength he had.

The back wall of the shed had been completely blown away in the blast and he dragged Molly out of it and across the ground away from the flames that had now taken hold. Then he lay down beside her in the smoke and ash-filled air, panting and trembling.

Molly was in a bad way; her fur was coated in blood and her breathing was ragged. The anxious young dog licked his friend's face and whimpered.

Chapter 2

Nathan Green had seen countless acts of human bravery since the war began, but he'd never seen a dog actually drag another dog to safety before.

The smaller one was lying very still, while the larger one kept licking and pushing at it. It was almost as if the bigger dog was trying to persuade its friend to wake up.

The house that had taken the direct hit had been cleared and the fires it had started in the houses on either side put out, although the soot and ash from the blast still filled the air, so Nathan headed over to the two dogs.

'Wait!' the elderly warden called after him. Nathan stopped. 'Don't go getting yourself bitten on your last night with us. A frightened animal's not going to be thinking straight.'

The warden was going to miss Nathan when he left. He was one of the best search-and-rescue volunteers they had ever had. But the boy was almost eighteen, even though with his slight frame he could pass for a much younger lad, and he'd recently received his call-up papers.

'I'll be careful, I promise,' Nathan said. He carried on towards the dogs as the animal rescue ambulance arrived.

Kate pulled on the ambulance's handbrake and grabbed her first-aid kit. Before the war she'd been a veterinary nurse. Now when the air raid sirens went off she became part of NARPAC, the National Air Raid Precautions Animal Committee.

'Don't you have a muzzle?' the warden

called after her, as he pointed to where Nathan and the dogs were.

'I'll make do with a bandage if I get worried about being bitten,' Kate replied. She never liked to use a muzzle unless she absolutely had to, because they could be very distressing for some dogs. The injured animal didn't look as if it would even be able to sit up, let alone bite her.

She ran to catch up with Nathan.

'At least the injured dog's got a NARPAC disc on its collar,' Kate said with relief as they got closer and she could see the distinctive white disc with a blue cross on it that all registered dogs wore.

'But what about the other dog, the one that rescued it?' Nathan asked.

'Doesn't look like he's got a collar on at all,' Kate said, avoiding his question. She'd seen Nathan before, helping at the bomb sites, but she didn't really know him.

'No,' Nathan agreed. It didn't.

The big dog's eyes never left Nathan and he didn't move away as Nathan approached him and his friend.

'Let's just concentrate on getting the injured dog some help for now. Someone will be sent for the other one in the morning,' Kate said, and she pressed her lips together to stop herself from saying more.

But Nathan was worried about the other dog. 'What happens to dogs that don't have a NARPAC disc on their collar?' he asked her.

Kate sighed and shook her head.

'We can't look after them all,' she said, but Nathan wasn't listening to her because he was looking at the big dog, who had stood up.

The German Shepherd took a few paces towards the young man, and then headed back to his friend, stopping every few moments to look behind him. The dog definitely wanted them to come and help but Kate was worried it might get in the way while she was trying to examine the smaller one.

'Here, try throwing a bit of this over that way,' she said, pulling a beef-dripping sandwich from her pocket. She'd been eating it for her tea when the siren went off and she'd had to dash out of the door without stopping to finish it. 'It'll distract the big dog so I can take a look at the injured one.'

Nathan threw the sandwich off to the side, where Kate had told him to. The dog watched the bread being thrown, looked at it, and then turned back to Nathan.

'One perfectly good sandwich wasted. Go on you silly dog, eat it!' Kate told him.

But all the dog did was look steadily back at them, then slowly raise his paw as if he were asking them to do something to help his friend. He wasn't leaving Molly, not even for food.

Kate and Nathan kept slowly walking towards the dogs.

'Be careful,' Kate told Nathan.

It didn't take long for a dog to turn from a house pet into a wild animal, some said only forty-eight hours or so.

'Young puppies need to be stroked frequently and held by human hands,' said Kate. 'If they don't get this, it's unlikely they'll ever become truly comfortable and relaxed as pets.'

'I will be careful,' answered Nathan.

As Nathan moved towards the dog, who'd been such a good friend to his injured pal, the dog backed away, unsure. He wasn't used to contact with people – other than being shouted at or having things thrown at him.

Kate gave Nathan her last sandwich and Nathan broke bits off it and crouched down so that he wouldn't be as frightening.

'Here dog, come here,' he called in a soft, non-threatening voice.

The young animal took a step towards him and then stopped. He stared at the hand that held the sandwich, glanced up at Nathan's face for a fraction of a second and then back at the sandwich. He was always very hungry and the sandwich was almost impossible to resist.

'He'll feel less threatened if you don't look directly at him,' Kate said over her shoulder, as she reached Molly.

Nathan knew the dog wanted the bit of sandwich because he could see it drooling, but would it be brave enough to come over to him? Nathan waited. The dog took another few paces forward but then stopped and sat down, his head tilted to one side as he looked at Nathan.

Nathan laughed. The dog was playing him at his own game!

He stood up and moved a few paces backwards, dropping small bits of sandwich on the ground as he did so. All the time he kept his head turned away from the dog, as Kate had suggested, but he could still just see any movement it made from the corner of his eye.

The dog took a step closer and then another. The sandwich lure was too strong to ignore.

He ate one bit of the sandwich and then he ate another. He didn't see Nathan smiling to himself. Nathan risked taking a step towards him and he scuttled a few feet away, then stopped.

'It's all right,' Nathan told the dog. 'Your friend's going to be all right.'

Every time Nathan moved forward the dog moved back, but he didn't try to interfere or stop Kate as she examined Molly and cleaned the cut on her head.

'Her wounds don't look too bad but I'll need to take her back to the clinic for a proper examination,' Kate said, and Nathan came over, with the other dog following a few steps behind.

'We can use my coat,' Nathan said, and he

pulled it off and laid it on the ground beside Molly.

Molly whimpered as Kate and Nathan slid her on to Nathan's coat and Nathan lifted her in his arms.

'She hardly weighs a thing,' he said.

Molly looked fragile and vulnerable. The big dog whined and followed them as they made their way back to the ambulance where the warden was waiting.

'What exactly happens to dogs that aren't registered?' Nathan asked Kate again as they reached the NARPAC ambulance.

Kate sighed. 'It's an impossible situation. There are already far too many homeless dogs – especially in Dover.'

Nathan felt a feeling of dread in the pit of his stomach.

'So what happens to them?' he repeated.

'Unregistered stray dogs are put down,' Kate said as she opened the ambulance door. 'It's not my choice,' she added when she saw Nathan's stricken face. 'But it's what we have to do.'

Nathan stared at the German Shepherd standing only a few paces away. He'd been so brave helping his friend. Nathan couldn't bear the thought of him being put down – it was so unfair. The dog shouldn't have to die just because it hadn't been registered. It wasn't right. He had to do something – couldn't let it happen – but he'd had his call-up papers and was due to leave for basic training in two days' time.

Nathan lifted Molly into the ambulance.

Her friend barked, not understanding what was happening or where they were taking Molly. He'd never been separated from her before.

'It's all right,' Nathan said. He reached out to stroke the dog without thinking, but it ducked out of the way.

'Seventeen Harold Road,' Kate read from the back of Molly's NARPAC collar.

'I'll let the owner know she's been found,' the warden said as he climbed on to his heavy single-speed bicycle.

'Thank you,' Kate said.

A major part of an animal rescuer's work, and the best part in Kate's opinion, was reuniting lost pets with their owners.

The German Shepherd looked up at Nathan and then back at Molly in the ambulance. He whined mournfully.

'Right, let's get her some medical attention as soon as possible. See you later, Nathan,' Kate added, then she closed the ambulance door and the big dog was left staring at the back of it as she ran round to the driver's side, jumped in and started the engine. The sooner she got Molly back to the clinic the better.

The German Shepherd barked, but the ambulance door didn't open. He barked again but it remained closed.

As the ambulance drove off he ran after it, ran and ran, until it was gone and he could run no more.

He threw back his head and howled in misery.

Chapter 3

He was lost without Molly. She'd always been there for him. She was the one who had decided where they should go and when they should eat – even where they slept at night. But now Molly was gone and he didn't know what to do. He sank down on to the road with his head on his paws, looking utterly despondent, and that's where Nathan found him.

'You can certainly run fast,' Nathan gasped, bending double as he tried to catch his breath.

Nathan's coat still had the faint scent of Molly on it. The dog looked up at him and whined.

'Don't worry, your friend's going to be OK,' Nathan told him, but he knew the dog couldn't understand. How could he?

He took a step closer but the big dog jumped up and moved to the other side of the road before turning and looking back at Nathan.

Nathan rummaged around inside his coat pocket and found a small leftover piece of the sandwich Kate had given him earlier. He threw it to the dog, who took a few steps forward to eat it, then just stood there, his tail between his legs. It seemed to Nathan that the dog's blue eyes were staring straight into his own brown ones, trying desperately to communicate with him.

'I don't have any more food,' Nathan explained, but the dog just kept on looking at him, willing him to understand.

When Kate arrived at the clinic with Molly she found it was as chaotic as usual. There were always far too many animals needing treatment for their injuries. Some of them had been hurt by bomb blasts, but many more had been wounded afterwards by falling debris or had cut their paws on broken glass or fragments of metal. Kate laid Molly down in one of the cubicles for the vet to examine her.

Molly's eyes opened and Kate could see the fear in them.

'It's all right, you're going to be just fine,' she said as she softly stroked the trembling dog.

Molly's eyes closed and she drifted back to sleep.

While Kate waited for the vet she filled in a brief report of what had happened at the site, but she left out the answer to one of the questions. She was supposed to report any dogs that had been spotted that weren't registered with NARPAC, so they could be collected, but Kate couldn't bear the thought that the dog that had stayed by his injured friend's side would be put to sleep without being given a chance, so she left out any mention of him.

'I'm Mrs Williams and I'm looking for my dog, Molly. She's a honey-coloured spaniel and the warden said she was here,' said an anxious voice outside the cubicles. 'Please tell me if she is. Please tell me, have you found my Molly?'

Kate swished back the curtain to find a middle-aged woman wearing a coat over her dressing gown and with house slippers on her feet, wringing her hands as she asked one of the other nurses about her dog.

'Have you found her?' the woman asked, turning to Kate. 'Please tell me it's true. I've been so worried about her. I miss her so. The house doesn't feel right without her.' She'd tied a scarf round her head to cover up the rollers in her hair, and knotted it under her chin. As she spoke, she nervously pushed back one of the rollers that had started to work its way free.

'She's in here,' Kate said, beckoning the woman over to the cubicle.

'Oh, Molly, dearest Molly,' Mrs Williams said as tears of worry and relief rolled down her face at the sight of her dog. 'Is she going to be all right?'

'Yes. She's been injured and was knocked unconscious – the vet still needs to see her – but I think she's going to be absolutely fine,' Kate reassured her.

'I blame myself for her getting lost,' Mrs Williams said. 'I should have told them Molly was still inside as soon as I'd been rescued after the house was struck by the bomb, just over a year ago now. But I didn't – not till they'd taken me away on the stretcher and I was lying in the ambulance. I'd been unconscious and wasn't thinking straight. They said they'd see to me first and I wasn't to worry, but I did worry and when they couldn't find her I thought she was . . . must be . . .' She couldn't bring herself to say the word 'dead', but another tear slipped down her face at the memory.

Molly opened her eyes at the sound of the familiar voice and her tail wagged slowly up and down once as if she were saying hello.

'She had a good friend with her when we found her,' Kate said. 'Another dog – an Alsatian – who stayed by her side when she was injured. Without him she may not have survived, but because of him she did. We don't know who he belongs to. I don't suppose there's any chance you'd be interested in giving him a home with you? He and Molly did seem very attached to each other.'

Mrs Williams blew her nose loudly on her handkerchief. 'Oh my goodness, dear, I couldn't possibly take on a dog that size at my age. I wish I could help but Molly is the only dog for me. How soon will she be allowed to come home?' she asked.

'She'll need the vet to check her over before we'll know that,' Kate told her. 'But I don't think it should be very long at all before she can go back home with you.'

'I have to get home,' Nathan told the dog. He'd given him all the food he had and there was nothing left.

Nathan started to walk away, but then something made him look back. The dog was following him! It wasn't brave enough to get too close though, and stopped when it was about a yard away.

Nathan walked on a bit further and then glanced behind him again. The dog was still there! Ten minutes later they reached Nathan's street and Nathan turned up the path to his house.

The house, like all the other houses they'd passed, had no lights that could be seen from the outside, because of the strict blackout. Any light that showed from the houses could be used by enemy bombers to work out where to target, so the lights-out rule was strictly enforced. Nathan pulled his key from its string around his neck and opened the door.

'I'm home, Mum,' he called out. He wasn't sure if she'd be back from her shift at the underground hospital at Dover Castle yet. She worked long and irregular hours there as an auxiliary nurse.

'Oh good, your supper's . . .' Mrs Green started to say, but then she saw the beast standing behind Nathan in the semi-darkness and she screamed and jumped on a chair. 'A wolf!'

'It's not a wolf, Mum. It's an Alsatian,' Nathan reassured her. 'No one seems to like to call them German Shepherd dogs because of the war, but they really are great dogs, Mum.' Nathan said. 'It's not their fault they've got that name. You should have seen how brave he was today.'

The dog looked from Nathan to his mother standing on a chair and back to Nathan. He tilted his head to one side, floppy ear down, and gave a small whine.

'What's it doing in our house?' Mrs Green asked, her voice higher than usual.

Nathan couldn't lie to her. 'It followed me home.'

'Well, it can't stay here,' Mrs Green said. 'You'll be going off in a couple of days.'

She didn't like the way it was looking at her. It looked hungry.

'Please, Mum,' Nathan said. 'Let him stay just for tonight. He saved his friend from a fire and then got left behind when they took her away.'

As if on cue the dog whined and sat down. He tilted his head to one side again as he looked up at her, almost as if he were adding his own plea.

Mrs Green climbed slowly down from the

chair. She'd always been a bit wary of big dogs, but since the war had started there'd been a lot of things she'd always been frightened of that she now found herself reconsidering. She was very much looking forward to the war being over, so everything could get back to normal.

'What's its name?' she asked.

'I don't know,' Nathan said. 'He doesn't have a collar.'

'Well, we'll have to call him something. Can't just call him Dog,' Mrs Green said. 'Doesn't feel right.'

Nathan looked down at the dog beside him. He was covered in soot and ash from the blast, as he was sure he must be himself.

'Grey?' he suggested.

His mother nodded and managed a nervous smile. 'Suits him,' she said.

Grey's tail flapped up and down.

'I know someone who'd like him very much,' Mrs Green said.

'Penny,' Nathan agreed.

His younger sister had been evacuated to keep her safe from the bombs.

Mrs Green remembered that she had a letter for Nathan from Penny. It had been in the same envelope as the one addressed to her.

'She sent this for you,' she said, pulling the letter from her dressing gown pocket.

She missed her daughter terribly, but as the shelling had increased, she'd had no choice but to send Nathan's ten-year-old sister to her parents' farm in Kent for safety.

Nathan smiled as he took the envelope from her. Penny had drawn a picture of herself waving whilst surrounded by farm animals.

'To the best big brother in the world. Make sure you sort out Mr Hitler and come home safe. I love you, Penny xxx.'

Mrs Green had stayed in Dover to continue to help the wounded soldiers who were brought to the underground hospital at the castle. It also meant she should have been able to see Nathan off, but she'd found out, as she was finishing her shift today, that that wasn't going to be possible.

'I've been put on earlies for the next week,' she said sadly, as Nathan read the letter from his sister. 'Sorry, love, it means I'll have to leave at five. I told them you were going but they've had an outbreak of flu, as if those poor wounded soldiers haven't got enough to put up with already, and I'm badly needed.'

'It's OK, Mum,' Nathan told her. He knew she'd have been there for him if she possibly could.

'What's Grey going to eat?' Mrs Green asked as she headed to the kitchen with Nathan and Grey following her. 'A big dog like that'll need a lot of food. The butcher's down the road is selling meat dyed green for dogs.'

She took Nathan's favourite dinner, steak and kidney pie, from the oven, and added some boiled potatoes and carrots to the plate. She'd been saving up her ration coupons ever since Nathan got his call-up papers so she could make it for him.

'He can have half my supper. I'm not very hungry,' Nathan lied, as he scraped half his dinner on to a tin plate and set it on the floor, then sat down at the kitchen table.

Mrs Green bit her bottom lip but didn't say anything as Grey gulped down the result of all her careful ration coupon saving in just a few seconds. Nathan had always been an animal lover and a generous son. If he wanted to share his special meal with this dog then that was up to him.

As he ate the rest of his steak and kidney pie, Nathan told his mum what had happened that evening.

'Grey howled when the ambulance took the other dog away, Mum. Actually howled, like a wolf,' he said.

Mrs Green looked down at Grey. He'd finished all the pie and licked his plate clean. He did remind her of a wolf.

'There used to be wolves in Britain, still are in parts of Europe,' she told Nathan as she sipped her last cup of tea of the day.

'I wish one would eat Mr Hitler and end the war for us,' Nathan said, spearing a boiled potato.

'A wolf would probably spit him out in disgust,' Mrs Green laughed and Nathan joined in.

Grey looked from one to the other, and then thoroughly licked his plate again, although there wasn't a scrap of food left on it.

'Where's Grey going to sleep?' Mrs Green asked, when Nathan had finished eating. She glanced towards the back door that led out to the garden, wondering whether they could use the Andersen shelter as a kennel for the night. But Nathan didn't think it was a good idea for

Grey to sleep out in the garden because he might run off.

'He can sleep in my room,' he said.

'Oh – oh, good,' Mrs Green said. She really hadn't fancied bumping into the dog when she came downstairs for her early morning cup of tea before setting off for the hospital.

'And where's he going to go once you've gone?' she asked, rather anxiously.

'Don't worry, Mum. I'll think of something,' said Nathan, sounding a lot more confident than he actually was.

'All right, night love,' she said, and she kissed Nathan on the forehead. 'I'll probably have left before you wake up in the morning.'

'I worry about you all alone here once I'm gone, Mum. What if something happens? I wish you could be with Penny,' Nathan said.

But Mrs Green shook her head. She couldn't do that. She was needed here. 'I'll be all right. Worse comes to the worst I can sleep up at the hospital or at the Esplanade caves if our house gets hit, which I'm sure it won't. Did you know, one of the soldiers told me today, those big guns Hitler's got aimed at us from across the Channel are so big a man could crawl inside the barrel and have room to take a kip – if he was inclined to sleep inside a gun that could shoot you all the way across the sea, that is.'

'I love you, Mum,' Nathan said softly.

'Love you too. I'm proud of you, son and don't you forget it.'

Grey tilted his head and watched her wipe her tears on the sleeve of her dressing gown as she left the room. 'And I'll miss you when you leave,' she added, but didn't tell him that she felt like her heart was breaking every time she thought of him going off to war.

'This way, Grey,' Nathan said.

He took Grey outside into their small garden

to do his business and then Grey followed him back inside.

Grey had never needed to go upstairs before and he stood at the bottom of them looking up at Nathan as he went.

'Come on Grey,' Nathan said, standing at the top of the stairs and patting his leg.

Grey whined, but then cautiously went up one stair and then another. The narrow steps were awkward for a dog of his size and he didn't find them at all easy. But at last he reached the top and wagged his tail with relief. He even let Nathan pat him for the first time.

Nathan put a blanket on the floor by his bed for Grey and Grey circled round it and scratched it before lying down. It was hard to get to sleep without Molly's warm body beside him.

Sometime during the night Grey climbed on to Nathan's bed and he was still there when Nathan woke up in the morning.

Chapter 4

Nathan didn't hear his mum standing outside his bedroom door at five o'clock the next morning, before she slipped quietly out of the house for her shift at the hospital, but Grey did. He was instantly awake and alert, but then he looked over at Nathan, still fast asleep, and dozed off again.

Two hours later, Nathan was awoken by the sound of Grey's snores. But almost as soon as Nathan opened his eyes, Grey was awake too, sitting up, fully alert, panting and staring at him.

'Good dog,' Nathan said, and Grey allowed himself to be stroked, although he still didn't seem to be completely comfortable being touched.

Nathan glanced over at his call-up papers and travel documents, which were sitting on the dresser beside his bed. Along with his call-up papers he'd received his ticket and details of his journey. There were an awful lot of stations between Dover and the basic training camp at Cardington, and it looked as though the train stopped at every one on their journey through Kent, London, Hertfordshire and Bedfordshire to their destination. Today was his last day as a civilian and he was going to spend it with Grey. He threw back the covers and climbed out of bed. Grey immediately jumped off too and padded after him.

His second experience of the stairs wasn't as bad as his first had been, but they still weren't easy for a big dog, and going down felt a lot trickier than going up.

Once they were safely downstairs, Nathan opened the back door to let Grey go outside and do his business. While Grey was sniffing the lavender bush, which was the neighbourhood tom cat's favourite haunt, Nathan carried the tin bath in from where it hung on a nail outside and set it in front of the kitchen range.

Next he set the kettle and a saucepan to heat on the range. Once they were piping hot, he poured them into the tin bath and then refilled them both to heat up again. He did this twice more until there was about three inches of water in the bottom of the bath.

Grey was still outside when Nathan stripped off his clothes and climbed in, but a moment later he was there, staring intently at him. The dog looked at the bath water, put his head down and drank some of it, sneezed a little at the surprising warmth of it, then sat down and gazed at Nathan holding the sponge.

Nathan found it very unnerving sitting naked in the tin bath with Grey staring at him. At times the dog tilted his head to one side and looked at him as if he was trying to work out what on earth was going on. Grey's coat had been covered in ash and soot the night before and it was matted and dirty. He looked as though he'd never had a bath in his life.

Nathan wasn't sure how Grey would react to being washed. Some dogs hated water and others loved it.

He stood up, stepped out of the bath and pulled a towel down from the kitchen pulley rack.

'In you go, Grey,' he said, pointing at the bathwater.

Grey bent his head and lapped at the water in the bottom of the tin bath again, but he didn't get in.

Nathan reached down and splashed his fingers about in the water.

'It's nice,' he said. 'Go on.' He pointed at the water again, but Grey clearly had no intention of getting in and stayed firmly where he was.

Nathan sighed. 'Sponge bath then.'

He dipped the sponge in the bathwater, rubbed coal tar soap on the sponge and then squeezed it over Grey's back. The soap certainly made Grey's fur smell a lot nicer than it had previously.

'That's it, you're OK,' he told Grey, as the dog turned to look with interest at the river of soapy suds running down his back. Nathan laughed. Grey did seem to be a bit bewildered by it all, but at least he wasn't running away.

Nathan lathered the soap deep into Grey's fur and then sponged it off with plenty of clean water. At last, all rinsed off, it was time to dry him.

However, before he could get another towel from the pulley rack, Grey started to shake himself vigorously and sprayed water everywhere; all over the walls, the range and the floor. Nathan did his best to mop it up, and then dried Grey as thoroughly as he could with the soggy towel.

Grey really seemed to like being dried; he made little sounds of happiness deep in his throat, which made Nathan smile. Before he'd washed him he'd thought Grey was mainly a dark charcoal grey all over, but now he found that parts of his coat were actually quite pale, and as the fur became properly dry he discovered that the dog was in fact sable coated.

'You really are a beautiful dog,' he told him. And judging by the way Grey held his head up proudly, he thought he'd probably agree.

'You know what you need? You need a brush,' Nathan said. Nathan himself used a comb on his hair and he didn't think his mother would appreciate him using her hairbrush on Grey, but the scrubbing brush turned out to be perfect. As he ran the bristle brush down Grey's sable coat he smoothed out any remaining matting and knots in his fur.

Grey lifted his head to encourage Nathan to concentrate on his favourite brushing place – under his chin.

'More there?' Nathan said as he obediently brushed the spot.

The dog's pointy ears – one grey and standing straight up, the other white-tipped and flopping down – were velvety soft, softer than the rest of his coat. Not that the rest of his coat was rough, especially after all the brushing, but it didn't have the buttery softness of his ears.

Nathan laughed when he was brushing the dog's tummy and found a tickle spot that made Grey sneeze.

He'd only known Grey a very short time but already he was starting to wish the dog could be his. But that wasn't possible because he was leaving for army basic-training camp tomorrow.

Nathan wished that Penny could meet Grey. She was crazy about dogs and he was sure she'd like him just as much as he did. But at least Penny was with animals at their grandparents' smallholding and it was a lot safer than Dover – Hellfire Corner, as everyone now called it because of all the damage it was receiving. Nathan was worried about leaving his mum alone. He wished she could join Penny and be safe. He wished they could have Grey with them to protect them, but he'd seen how frightened his mum was of Grey, even though she'd tried to hide it.

'Hungry?' Nathan asked the dog. Nathan certainly was. Grey padded close behind him as Nathan went to see what there was in the pantry.

'Sit!' Nathan said as he opened the pantry door and reached inside.

Grey looked at Nathan, then at the bit of chicken in Nathan's hand and back at Nathan.

'Sit!' Nathan said again.

But Grey didn't. Nathan wasn't even sure that Grey understood what the word meant, and he didn't want to frighten him by trying to push his bottom to the ground.

Nathan sat down on the kitchen floor.

'Sit!'

Grey looked at the chicken and then at Nathan. He sat down.

'Good dog!' Nathan cried, and he gave him the piece of chicken, which Grey gulped down in a single swallow, seemingly without chewing it at all.

Nathan scrambled to his feet to get more chicken and Grey stood up and followed him. He wasn't quite sure what it was he'd done to get the chicken but he definitely wanted more.

'Sit!' Nathan said, and his hand unconsciously lifted as he said it.

Grey watched Nathan's movement, looked at the chicken and sat.

'Yes!' Nathan said as Grey gulped down the food. The dog was a quick learner, at least when there was chicken involved. Maybe the dog had been taught the command before, maybe he had once had a family, Nathan didn't know.

He wanted to take Grey for a walk but he didn't even have a collar or a lead for him. He improvised by making an extra hole in his own belt to use as a collar and used the washing line, doubled over a few times, as a lead.

At first, Grey backed away when Nathan tried to put the collar on, but Nathan dropped a scrap of bread on the floor, and while Grey was busy gobbling it up Nathan managed to get the collar safely buckled around his neck. He threaded the washing line through the belt as a makeshift lead. Grey looked unimpressed.

'Come on now,' Nathan said. 'You have to wear it.'

When Nathan tried to get Grey to go the way he wanted him to go, Grey didn't like it at all and started to pull in the opposite direction.

'This way,' Nathan said, holding out more bread to Grey. 'Bread doesn't grow on trees you know,' he murmured as they headed out of the house and down the road.

Grey just gave him a look, but then he caught sight of the park just ahead. He was very fond of running on grass and chasing squirrels and he dragged Nathan towards the park so hard that he had to cling on to the lead with both hands.

'Whoa, slow down there, stop,' he pleaded.

But Grey wasn't listening. He was a strong dog who knew where he wanted to go, and as soon as they reached the park, in they went.

Grey ran fast and Nathan had no choice but to let go of the lead or end up being dragged into a hawthorn bush.

As he watched Grey run on without him, Nathan worried that he was going to lose him. What if the dog didn't come back?

He spotted a ball that had been left half hidden under the bush and picked it up.

'Grey, Grey, Grey . . .' he yelled, as he waved his hands in the air.

The dog stopped for a moment to look over at him but didn't come back.

'Fetch!' Nathan threw the ball into the air. Grey followed it with his eyes and the next moment he was running across the grass chasing after it.

He'd never played ball before but he liked it just as much as chasing squirrels, and he soon got the idea that if he brought it back to Nathan then Nathan could make it fly through the air for him to chase all over again.

Nathan soon found out that when it came to meeting other dogs, Grey wasn't the least bit wary. Nathan watched as he bounded over to the other dogs in the park, wagging his tail to sniff and say hello.

Most of the dog owners were happy to see him, but some owners, especially those with little dogs, were frightened and quickly picked up their pets for safety.

'Looks like he could eat my Trixie for breakfast . . .'

'I'm sure he wouldn't,' Nathan replied.

'Don't want Puddle getting injured by those big paws . . .'

'He's quite gentle, really,' Nathan said.

'My, but you've got a big dog there. I bet the War Dog Training School would like a few more like him.'

Nathan hadn't heard of the War Dog Training School before.

'What's that?' he asked.

But the lady didn't know much about it. 'There was an advert in the paper. They're looking for dogs to train up for the war effort.'

Nathan looked down at Grey, who gazed up at him and then down at his ball.

'Where is this War Dog Training School?' Nathan asked the lady. 'Is it around here?'

'No, it isn't local. Let me see. It was somewhere I haven't been . . . Hampshire, Herefordshire . . . no . . . oh, I remember, it was Hertfordshire.'

Nathan threw the ball for Grey who raced after it but then he spotted a honey-coated spaniel, a lot like Molly, way across the other side of the park and he went racing over to it.

'Grey, Grey, come back!' Nathan called as he ran after him.

The dog wasn't Molly, and worse still the owner looked at Grey in horror and dragged his own dog away.

'Keep that brute away from my dog,' he shouted at Nathan.

'He was just coming to say hello,' Nathan said reasonably. 'He thought . . .' But the man didn't let him finish. 'Dogs like him don't think – they just attack without warning,' he said, and stomped off.

Nathan looked down at Grey and sighed. 'I suppose to some people you might look a bit dangerous.'

Grey tilted his head to one side and looked up at him. 'But not once they get to know you, of course,' Nathan added.

Grey panted as he watched the spaniel being dragged out of the park. Nathan was sure he had run over to the dog because he'd hoped it might be his friend.

'Come on,' he said, picking up Grey's lead. The Houghton Street Clinic, where Molly had been taken, wasn't far away. 'Let's see how she's getting on.'

Kate was stunned to see them both when they arrived.

'Isn't that the dog from last night?' she asked.

Nathan nodded as Grey sat down next to

him. 'We came to see how his friend was getting on,' Nathan added.

'Molly went home with her owner this morning,' Kate said. 'Both of them looked over the moon to be reunited. Molly will need to take it easy for the next few days, but I'm sure she'll be getting lots of cuddles and love and will be better in no time.' She looked down at Grey. 'He looks like you gave him a bath.'

'I did. Do you think maybe someone would take him on now? Only I would, I really would, but I'm off to basic training tomorrow.'

Kate shook her head. 'I'm sorry,' she said. 'But no one's taking on any stray dogs, not in wartime.'

Nathan understood but he still felt bad. It wasn't the dog's fault that they were at war.

He remembered the woman in the park mentioning the War Dog Training School.

'Have you heard about the War Dog Training School?' he asked. 'Could he go there? I bet he'd make a great war dog.'

Kate nodded. 'There's a poster about it on the wall over there. A big, healthy young dog like him might be lucky and get selected.'

'Whereabouts in Hertfordshire is it?' Nathan asked her, as Grey watched with interest as other dogs and cats were brought in and taken out of the clinic doors in a seemingly never-ending stream.

'Place called Potters Bar,' she told him. 'But they'd expect him to be able to walk to heel and have some basic obedience skills.'

'I can teach him those,' Nathan said.

'I bet you could,' Kate replied. 'He certainly does seem to like you. Wait here a minute.'

She hurried off as Nathan read the 'War Dogs Wanted' poster and Grey sniffed at passing dogs.

A few moments later, Kate returned with a proper collar and lead for Grey.

'These'll be better than a belt and washing-line string,' she said kindly.

'Thanks,' said Nathan as he put them on Grey. The dog didn't seem to mind, and seemed to have got used to the idea of wearing a collar already.

'Good luck,' she said.

Nathan was the best chance the dog had of not being put down.

For the rest of the morning Grey practised walking to heel and Nathan was very pleased with how quickly the dog learnt what he was supposed to do.

'You are one clever dog,' he told Grey, and Grey wagged his tail.

Nathan was shocked when a few minutes later, as they were walking down the street, two children saw Grey and started screaming: 'It's a wolf, it's a wolf!'

'He's not a wolf,' Nathan called after them as they ran away in panic, but they didn't stop to discover the truth. Nathan was still upset by this encounter when suddenly something even worse happened. A scruffy-looking older boy threw a chunk of brick from a bomb site at Grey and it only just missed him. If it had been a couple of inches to the right, he would have been seriously hurt.

'Hey!' Nathan yelled at the boy. 'What do you think you're doing?'

'Nazi dog deserved it,' the boy sneered.

'He isn't a Nazi . . .' Nathan started to say, but the boy ran off around the nearest corner and quickly disappeared from view.

Nathan looked down at Grey, and Grey looked up at him with his gentle blue eyes.

'They won't even give you a chance to show what a great dog you are,' he said. It just seemed so unfair. But at least perhaps they'd give Grey a chance at the War Dog Training School and, as luck would have it, Potters Bar was one of the stations his train would be stopping at on the way to his basic training camp at Cardington, so he could drop Grey off on the way.

Chapter 5

Grey's tail hung low as they went into Dover Priory train station. It smelt strange, and the hustle and bustle of the travellers and station staff worried him. For most of his life he'd stayed as far away from people as he could possibly get, but here they were everywhere.

Nathan, holding tightly to his brown cardboard suitcase, looked down at Grey, sensing his distress.

'It's OK,' he said in an attempt soothe him, trying to be calm for the benefit of the dog, but inside he was starting to worry that taking Grey on a train might not be such a good idea. Grey was a stray, after all. What if he bit someone, or ran on to the tracks in terror?

Grey looked up at Nathan, his eyes wide with fear, and Nathan remembered hearing how a dog could sense its owner's emotions down its lead. Nathan had been gripping the lead Kate had given him very tightly, so tightly that his knuckles were white. Now he realized he was probably making everything worse for Grey, and for himself. He took a long deep breath and let it out as slowly as he could. Then he shrugged a few times to loosen his shoulders and bent his head from left to right to release his own tension. Only then did he crouch down so that he was at Grey's eye level and stroke him.

Grey licked his hand and pushed his head into Nathan and gave a half wag of his tail, only to jerk away suddenly at the roar of the train as it approached.

Nothing Nathan did could stop Grey from shaking in absolute terror as the train steamed into the station. All the dog wanted to do was get away from it, and get Nathan away from it too.

He pulled on the lead but Nathan didn't come. He twisted and turned as he struggled wildly, and Nathan almost lost his grip on the lead, but he just managed to cling on.

'You've got to get on the train,' he said, desperately. 'You've got to get on, Grey, please. It's my only chance to save you.'

He remembered his grandfather telling him how nervous horses were moved in a circle and now he tried this with Grey, almost running, but also worrying that the train would leave without them.

'In here,' shouted a voice from the back of the train, and Nathan ran as fast as he could, followed by a surprised Grey, then jumped into the guard's van, and before he knew it Grey was in the guard's van too, the door was slammed shut, there was a piercing blast from the whistle and the train set off.

'Thanks,' Nathan said, to the junior guard who'd let them in.

''S OK, where are you two off to, then?'

'The War Dog Training School,' Nathan told him.

'Going to be an army pooch, is he? Well, he'll have to get used to a lot worse than a huffing puffing steam train.'

Nathan nodded his agreement.

Grey stood there panting with his tongue hanging out, until the wobbles and jolts from the train as it picked up speed caused him to swiftly sit down. But he carried on panting anxiously to show he wasn't happy and he didn't want to be here, not one little bit.

The guard's van didn't have a seat as it was designed to carry bicycles and wheelchairs. Nathan sat down on the floor next to Grey, who rested his head on his legs as Nathan stroked him.

They had to change trains at King's Cross, but this time when they got to the platform the steam train was already there waiting, the air was thick with clouds of steam and ringing with the clank of engines moving in and out of the platforms.

This time Nathan waited with Grey at the very back of the platform, as far away from the rails and the incoming and outgoing trains on other platforms as he could get, until it was time for them to board.

'It's all right,' he said as he stroked the big dog's head, but Grey didn't agree. His tail stayed firmly down and he pressed himself close into Nathan.

'Fine-looking dog,' said an elderly man who was holding a briefcase and wearing a colonel's uniform, nodding at Grey.

'Thanks,' Nathan said, 'I'm taking him to

the War Dog Training School to see if he can be a war dog.'

'Are you indeed?' the colonel said, and he gave a half smile. 'I wish you the very best of luck.'

'This way,' Nathan said to Grey when the train doors were finally opened.

Nathan headed briskly towards an open carriage door with Grey trotting beside him, but as they reached the steps to climb on, Grey showed Nathan he'd much rather not get on board by pulling back on his lead and whining.

Nathan thought quickly. He walked Grey round in a wide circle away from the train and back again at a quick pace, talking to him all the time, and then he pulled the ball he'd found at the park from his pocket, knowing how much Grey liked it, and as Grey reached his head out for it Nathan hurried up the steps.

Grey was so surprised and distracted by the sight of the ball that before he knew it he was in the carriage and lying on the ground at Nathan's feet with his ball in front of him.

The elderly colonel had been watching them from the window. 'Nicely handled,' he commented as Nathan sat down in the seat opposite.

Grey shook again as the train engine roared into life and they set off. He heaved a sigh, then whined quietly, but Nathan gave him some of the corned beef sandwich he'd brought with him for their lunch and Grey gulped it down. Nathan smiled.

'Not too frightening to put you off your food, then?' he said as Grey looked up at him, hoping for more food. 'There you go.' Nathan gave him the last crust of the bread. 'That's the lot.'

'Have you had him since he was a pup?' the colonel asked Nathan, as he pulled his own sandwiches from his briefcase.

Grey looked at the colonel's sandwiches with keen eyes.

'No, I haven't,' Nathan said, and he told the colonel the story of how he and Grey had met.

'Well, he's really taken a liking to you,' the older man said. 'Quite remarkable in such a brief period of time.'

'And me to him, sir,' Nathan said. 'I'm going to miss him terribly once I've dropped him off today.'

'And he'll miss you,' the colonel said thoughtfully, as he broke off some of his sandwich and gave it to Grey. 'Probably even more so.'

Grey gulped down the food and looked up at the colonel to see if there was any more.

'That's your lot, I'm afraid,' the colonel said as he took out his penknife and sliced off a piece of apple. Grey looked at the apple and drooled.

The colonel frowned and then offered the slice to Grey who immediately ate it.

'I didn't know dogs ate apples,' Nathan grinned.

'Doesn't do them any harm – unless they eat

too many and get a stomach ache, of course. I think your dog is so used to fending for himself that he'll try most things,' the colonel said. 'He'd be a useful dog to have on a reconnaissance trip – he'd find food if anyone could.'

The colonel looked thoughtful. 'You're off to do your basic training at the Cardington camp, you say?'

'Yes, sir.'

By the time they arrived at Potters Bar, where the colonel also got off, nearly two hours later, Grey was much more at home travelling by train and had even had a brief a nap on board.

The station staff gave Nathan directions to the old greyhound racing stables that had been taken over by the War Dog Training School.

As they walked there, Grey sniffed at the Hertfordshire air, which smelt much less salty than the air of Dover and much less steamy than the steam train.

Nathan stopped at the school's entrance gate.

'Name?' asked the young soldier standing on guard beside it.

'Er, Nathan Green, and this is Grey,' Nathan said. 'But we're not expected.'

'Right,' the soldier said, looking down at Grey who was now sitting with his head tilted to one side as he looked up at him, one ear standing up and the other flopping over.

The War Dog Training School hadn't been running for very long but it had seen a lot of dogs, of all sorts, come and go. When the public had been asked to lend their dogs to the war effort, tens of thousands had been offered, but less than half of them had been found to be even vaguely suitable.

A lot of the dogs with potential had been German Shepherds like Grey, so even though the dog handlers complained about being overwhelmed with offers of unsuitable dogs, the soldier knew they'd want to see this one.

'Hang on a minute and I'll get someone,' he said.

Grey lay down to wait.

Donated dogs were supposed to have been examined and registered by one of the animal welfare charities before being shipped to the War Dog Training School, but Nathan and Grey had arrived unexpectedly and with no papers. It was sometimes difficult to tell which dogs would make good military dogs and which wouldn't. But some tell-tale signs remained the same whatever duty the dogs were asked to do.

Very timid dogs usually had to be rejected during the initial stages. Those that were overly aggressive towards other dogs or people weren't good candidates either. Nor were dogs that were very protective of their food and growled at anyone who came close to their bowl. Or those that were the same when it came to a toy or a ball.

What the school was looking for in a military service dog was an animal with a friendly, biddable nature, but not one that was too soft and rolled over on its back to show its belly as soon as anyone approached, and not one that continually wandered off to greet strangers. So far they'd found most German Shepherds, or Alsatians as they were now known, to be intelligent and loyal with a good temperament. They were also easily trained and had a high level of endurance.

'I think you'll want to see this one,' the soldier on duty at the gate told his sergeant. 'There's something special about him.'

Michael Ward, the newest member of the dog handling team, was sent over to Nathan and Grey with the paperwork that needed to be filled out.

'Who's this, then?' Michael asked, as he

crouched down and patted Grey. Grey wagged his tail and nuzzled his head into him. Michael smelt of all the dogs he'd stroked that day, which was a lot.

'I call him Grey,' Nathan said.

'So Grey, you want to be an army dog, do you?' Grey sniffed at Michael's pocket and Michael laughed. 'Well, we can't expect you to work for nothing can we?' He pulled a biscuit from his pocket and Grey wolfed it down gratefully.

Over a strong cup of tea Nathan told Michael the story of how he and Grey had met.

'Doesn't look much like a stray, does he?' Michael observed, looking at the shiny-coated dog. 'Bit thin, of course, but nice coat and teeth and good clear eyes.'

'I gave him a bath before we left this morning,' Nathan grinned.

'You gave a stray adult dog a bath – and he let you?' Michael said, looking astonished.

'You're a braver man than I am. Ever thought about becoming a dog handler for the army? You seem to have a knack.'

Grey gazed up at Nathan as Michael looked down at Grey.

'And I can see that Grey thinks the world of you. Usually the first few weeks are spent building a bond between dog and handler, but you two have already got that,' Michael said.

Nathan pulled his call-up papers from his pocket.

'Unfortunately I can't, although I would if I could. If you could just give him a chance,' Nathan said.

'Don't worry yourself,' Michael told him. 'I can see he's a special dog and your affection for him just confirms that. I'll make sure he gets a fair trial.'

'Will you be his handler?' Nathan asked hopefully.

Michael shrugged. 'I don't know – probably

not. There are so many dogs here, but I'll keep a special eye on him whether I'm his handler or not.' He put down his teacup. 'Do you want to see where he's going to sleep?'

'Sure.' Nathan got to his feet and Grey immediately responded by standing up too.

He was very interested in the different smells coming from the camp and the dogs in the kennels. So long as Nathan was with him it was all interesting and he trotted along beside him, his tail up confidently.

Nathan stared at the rows of wooden dog kennels. It looked like an army barracks for canines. There was a lot of noise coming from them as dogs barked and whined, some of them standing up on their hind legs to watch the newcomers as they passed their doors. Grey looked interested, sniffed at some of the dogs and wagged his tail, but jumped back from a snarling Yorkshire terrier.

'Some of these dogs are here to be assessed

but others are being trained as guard dogs, tracker dogs and infantry dogs and also messenger dogs,' Michael told Nathan. 'That little Yorkie looks like it should be a guard dog. It'd see anyone off.'

'What are tracker and infantry dogs?' Nathan asked.

'Tracker dogs are given the scent of someone or something and trained to find it. Infantry dogs are trained to silently alert troops to an enemy danger by looking in the direction of the sound and not barking,' Michael told him. 'Then there are the messenger dogs. Some dogs can take messages between handlers up to eight miles apart, but one mile is usually the maximum distance the army expects from them.'

'Sounds like we need a lot of dogs,' Nathan said, and Michael grinned.

'There's even talk of some of them being trained as parachute dogs,' he said.

Nathan gave him a look of utter disbelief.

'It's true,' Michael insisted.

Nathan shook his head. 'No one can possibly expect a dog to jump out of a plane hundreds of feet up in the air. That's just crazy.'

'Maybe. But I'd love to be a paratrooper, wouldn't you? I can just imagine it.'

Nathan shook his head because he didn't want to imagine it. He'd been terrified of heights ever since he'd fallen off the garden shed when he was eight.

'I don't think there'll be many dogs that'd make the paratroop grade,' Michael said, wistfully, as he stopped beside an empty kennel. 'This one can be Grey's. We'll soon find out what job he's most suitable for once he's passed his assessment.'

'Do you really think he's got a chance, then?' Nathan asked.

'Yes, I do,' Michael told him. 'He's interested in what's going on around him, taking it all in. I'd say he's a smart dog.'

Nathan gave Grey one last stroke. 'You be a good dog,' he told him. 'You show them just what a good dog you are, OK?' His voice caught in his throat as Grey looked him directly in the eye. It was almost as if he knew he was being left behind all over again. But Nathan didn't have a choice. Call-up papers couldn't be ignored and he was going to be late if he didn't leave soon. 'I've got to go.'

'He'll be fine,' Michael said.

Chapter 6

Grey watched Nathan until he turned the corner and he couldn't see him any more. Then he looked up at Michael and whined, then looked back to the spot where he'd last seen Nathan.

Once out of sight, Nathan wiped his eyes on his sleeve. He was going to miss Grey, but he was sure he was in good hands with Michael.

'He's in the best place,' he told himself. But Grey didn't agree.

He barked in the direction Nathan had gone and when that didn't bring him back he pulled free from Michael's grasp and ran after Nathan, barking frantically, with Michael running behind him, yelling: 'Grey, come back!'

Nathan was almost at the exit of the War Dog Training School when Grey reached him.

'You can't come,' he said to the dog as Grey wagged his tail in delight at having found him. 'You've got to go back.' He pointed back the way he'd come and to Michael running towards them.

Grey whined. Then he sat down, cocked his head to one side and looked up at Nathan, unsure of what he'd done wrong, but knowing it must be something serious by Nathan's tone of voice.

Michael took hold of Grey's lead. 'Come on,' he said. 'You'll like it here, I promise.'

But Grey didn't think he would, and he struggled so hard against his lead that Michael had to virtually drag him away, his claws scrabbling on the road in an attempt to get a grip.

Nathan bit his bottom lip, then turned and headed out of the camp. He needed to get to Cardington by 4 p.m. and it was a twenty-minute walk to Potters Bar station.

He couldn't afford to be late so he lengthened his stride until he was almost running. The train station was just ahead but as he dashed down the steps to the platform, he heard a happy bark and Grey came bounding up to him, wagging his tail like crazy and looking very pleased with himself for having tracked him down again. Nathan couldn't even begin to imagine how the dog had been able to find him, let alone be allowed into the station.

'No, Grey,' Nathan said sternly, but something in his voice told Grey that Nathan didn't really mean it and he nudged his head under Nathan's hand for a stroke.

'You know, I think that dog would have followed you to the ends of the earth,' called a voice from the top of the steps.

'I'm sorry, sir,' Nathan said, registering with astonishment that the voice belonged to the colonel they'd met on the train. He went back up the steps with Grey following him, tail wagging.

'Well don't be. It's just the kind of devotion I'm looking for in my war dogs.'

Nathan was confused. 'Sir?'

'Lieutenant Colonel Richardson,' the colonel said, holding out his hand. 'I run the War Dog School and am looking for a dog exactly like yours – one that will do anything to please its handler.'

'But I'm not his handler,' Nathan said.

'Well, he certainly seems to think you're supposed to be his handler and he's the one that matters to me,' the colonel said. 'I've spoken to the chaps at Cardington and they've agreed to my commissioning you to work for our lot. You'll be reporting to me from now on.'

Nathan looked down at Grey, hardly able to believe what was happening. Could it really be possible that they weren't going to be separated after all?

'Right, sir,' he grinned. He couldn't think of a better way to spend the war than with Grey by his side.

'Get in, then,' the colonel said as they left the station. He pointed to the back of the jeep that he'd driven Grey in so that he could be there when he told Nathan the news.

Nathan climbed in and Grey immediately jumped in too and gave Nathan's face a lick once he'd sat down and was at the right level for him to do so.

'It'll be hard work, mind,' Lieutenant Colonel Richardson said as they drove back to the War Dog Training School. 'You'll be expected to do your basic training on top of your dog handling.'

'That's OK,' Nathan smiled. It'd be more than worth it if it meant that he and Grey could stay together.

'And make sure you massage his ears, especially the base of them,' the colonel added. 'They should both be standing up by now, not one up and one down.'

'Yes, sir.'

In a few minutes they were back at the school and Nathan and Grey climbed out of the jeep.

The colonel watched Grey as he headed off with Nathan. The dog had a lot of potential and with the boy handling him he was sure they could go far. They looked like they were already a team, definitely so as far as the dog was concerned, and he was the one that counted most. Nathan would get far more from him than even their most experienced handlers could, because Grey would want to do all that Nathan asked of him.

There was a lot of secret reconnaissance work needed prior to the D-Day mission to free France and the colonel was on the lookout for a dog that could parachute into France with his handler. Most dogs wouldn't be suitable and it would demand absolute trust in Nathan from the dog. But Grey just might be one of those rare dogs they were seeking and for covert work it helped that Nathan looked much younger than his age and might not be immediately identified as a soldier if they were unlucky enough to be caught.

'Welcome to the team,' Michael said, coming to join them. He slapped Nathan on the back as Grey wagged his tail, and they headed back to the kennel area together.

All the dog kennels had chains attached to them because the army couldn't have the dogs wandering about as they pleased, unsupervised.

This also prevented any dog fights. Nathan clipped the chain to Grey's collar and followed Michael over to the soldier's barracks.

Grey whined as Nathan left him. He tried to follow him but the chain stopped him. He sat down, then lay down and then finally stood up again, fretfully.

There were hundreds of new smells and new sounds to take in all around him. But he was only interested in getting Nathan back.

A short while later Nathan did come back and brought with him a tin bowl full of corned beef, vegetables and dog biscuits. He placed the food in front of Grey who gobbled it all up eagerly and then had a long drink of water.

Once he'd finished eating, Nathan took Grey for a walk around the camp to give him some extra lead-walking practice before his assessment the next day. Michael and a Border collie called Topper, who had also arrived that day and was going to be assessed too, came to join them.

'Try varying your pace,' Michael suggested to Nathan. And Nathan did, sometimes running and sometimes walking slowly. Grey thought this was a great new game as he matched his pace to his friend's.

Michael showed Nathan how to give a hand signal when he wanted Grey to go to the left or to the right. Grey soon got the idea of what he was supposed to do.

'You're a quick learner, dog,' Nathan told him, and Grey wagged his tail.

'He is indeed one smart dog,' Michael agreed. 'Can he stay if you tell him to?'

Nathan didn't know. 'Sit,' he said, and Grey obediently sat. 'Stay,' Nathan told him.

Nathan moved a few paces away and Grey immediately stood up to go after him. But that wasn't what Nathan wanted him to do. 'No!' Grey cocked his head to one side, unsure of what he'd done wrong. Nathan went back to him.

'Sit.'

Grey sat.

'Stay!' Nathan said, and he held his hand up with the palm facing the dog to show him what he meant.

Then Nathan stepped back a few paces, his eyes staring intently into Grey's blue ones, his palm still facing him. Grey made the tiniest of movements to go to him and immediately Nathan repeated, 'Stay.'

Grey stayed where he was and a few moments later Nathan came back to him and patted him and told him what a good dog he was.

They practised a few more times until Nathan could walk ten paces away and stay there for thirty seconds before returning to him. Grey knew he'd done well when Nathan knelt down and praised him. He nuzzled his face into Nathan's and then lifted his chin so Nathan could scratch under it.

Michael was very impressed. 'He really is a quick learner. He's bound to pass the test tomorrow – so long as he doesn't panic at all the loud noises and thunder flashes and what-not.'

'Does it matter that he's got one floppy ear?' Nathan asked. Most of the other German Shepherds he'd seen so far today had ears that went straight up. Even the colonel had commented on it.

'I think his ears are the least of his worries,' Michael grinned. 'Bit of good feeding will probably sort that out.'

When Nathan left him at his kennel for the night, Grey expected him to come back again at first. He watched for him and stood up every time someone went past. But finally he lay down on the blanket inside his kennel and went to sleep.

Back at the barracks, Nathan wrote to his mother to tell her he wasn't now going to be doing his basic training at Cardington. He was going to be Grey's dog handler at the War Dog Training School. Then he lay down on his bunk bed, but couldn't get to sleep. He was worrying about what would happen if Grey didn't pass his assessment in the morning. What if the dog was frightened of loud noises, understandably enough, or wouldn't perform on the day? It was expecting a lot from a dog who'd only just been taught to sit and stay.

Nathan rolled over and thumped his lumpy pillow to try and make it a bit more comfortable. Whatever happened tomorrow he was now a dog handler at the War Dog Training School. But what if Grey didn't pass? As an unregistered stray dog, the death sentence was still hanging over him if he failed and Nathan just couldn't bear the thought. Grey had to pass, he had to. He didn't want to be a dog handler if Grey couldn't be his dog. He didn't want to be in the army if Grey couldn't be in it too.

Grey was awake early the next morning, like all the other dogs, and overjoyed when he saw

Nathan heading towards him. He barked to tell him to hurry up and then put his paws on Nathan's shoulders and licked his face as soon as Nathan had got inside his kennel.

'OK, OK,' Nathan laughed. 'I'm glad you're pleased to see me.'

He filled up Grey's water tin with fresh water and Grey lapped at it with his long pink tongue. After a short walk it was time for Grey to be brushed. As the brush ran down his back Grey stretched up his head for more, reminding Nathan not to forget the place under his chin. Nathan smiled. By the time he'd finished brushing Grey's coat, it shone. Grey put his paw out to Nathan to ask him to continue brushing.

Nathan remembered what the colonel had said about massaging Grey's ears and soon found that Grey loved having the base of his ears massaged and almost purred with happiness as Nathan did it.

Chapter 7

Nathan clipped the army-issue chain lead to Grey's new collar, with its ID tag that had Grey's name on it, and led Grey, tail wagging, over to the training field.

It was important that the dogs being assessed were surprised by the different sounds of battle rather than expecting them. That way their reactions to them would show how they would react on a real battlefield. Colonel Richardson himself came to oversee Grey's assessment. He nodded to Nathan that he should start playing with Grey, and Nathan threw Grey's ball.

'Fetch!'

Grey never needed to be asked twice when it came to his ball. Once he was running after it the colonel signalled to another soldier who shot a pistol into the air.

Grey looked over at where the loud 'crack' sound had come from, but then went back to the more important task of chasing his ball.

It was just the reaction the colonel was looking for. A dog who kept on with what he was supposed to be doing even when there was gunfire going on around him.

'Good dog,' he muttered, as he put a tick in the first box on his sheet. If Grey had been frightened by the loud noise he'd have had to put a cross. It would have been fine, however, if Grey had been startled by the noise, just so long as he had recovered quickly and gone back to the task he'd been asked to do.

He nodded to Nathan and Nathan threw the ball for Grey again, and again Grey raced after it.

The colonel signalled to the soldier who'd fired the pistol. This time the soldier made a lot more noise with a pistol, firecrackers and finally a grenade.

Grey looked over at all the commotion, but it didn't stop him picking up the ball and bringing it back to Nathan.

The sounds of guns, bombs, air-raid sirens and the clattering of bells as ambulances and fire engines rushed to the scenes of bombings had been everyday occurrences in Dover. Grey accepted the sounds of violence that the soldier made as just the way things were.

He dropped the ball at Nathan's feet and wagged his tail. Nathan threw the ball again.

The colonel put a second tick on Grey's chart and signed and dated it at the bottom.

Grey had passed the initial assessment and

was now officially part of the War Dog Training School. He'd been able to concentrate while under fire and everything else he needed to learn they could work on. Nathan was over the moon and kept stroking Grey.

Grey wagged his tail because he liked Nathan stroking him. But then he looked pointedly at the ball. He wanted to play!

Over the next week Grey's love of his ball also helped with his scent and tracking training.

Nathan hid the ball all round the camp and then got Grey to seek it out. At first Nathan made finding the ball really easy and gave Grey lots of praise whenever he did find it. But Grey so obviously liked playing hide-and-seek and was so excited when he found the ball that soon Nathan was making it harder and harder to find, until Grey had to look round the whole camp for it. The game was Grey's first step in learning to track.

As well as playing hide and seek with the ball, Grey also learnt how to find people.

'Stay,' Nathan told him, and Grey waited with Michael or one of the other handlers while Nathan went and hid.

A few minutes later Grey was given the command: 'Find him!' and released.

It always took him less time to find Nathan than it had taken Nathan to hide. However well he thought he'd hidden, Grey's nose would sniff him out. Whenever he was successful Nathan was full of praise and hugs and treats, as Grey stood there wagging his tail, as pleased as punch with himself. Then they'd usually have a game of ball.

'One well-trained dog is as effective as twenty human trackers,' the colonel said. 'A dog's nose can pick up a human scent from five hundred yards away, if the conditions are right. On a good day, with the wind in the right direction, maybe even further.'

The colonel was very pleased with Grey's progress, and had discussed him with the commander of the paratroop regiment.

It was only a small step from being a tracker dog to taking messages between people. Grey obediently took messages from Nathan to Michael. But he was always much quicker when Michael wanted him to take a message to Nathan. Then he would race to find his friend.

Nathan often used ball play as a reward for Grey at the end of a good day's work. As Grey always worked hard and did his best, this meant that almost every day, rain or shine, would end with a game of ball. So much so that Grey came to expect it and was very disappointed and whined, giving Nathan pitiful looks, if it didn't happen.

'But it's raining!' Nathan said in response to Grey's reaction at the end of their second week at War Dog School. Grey clearly didn't think a little rain should stop him from playing.

'And not just raining a little,' Nathan laughed. The April shower had quickly turned torrential.

Grey barked.

'No, you don't tell me what to do,' Nathan said, his face breaking into a grin. 'It's the other way round.'

Grey picked up his ball and then dropped it on the ground and looked up at Nathan. His meaning couldn't have been clearer.

Nathan sighed. 'OK, OK,' he said. 'But if I catch a cold from playing ball in the rain I'm not going to be happy.' He was glad the colonel wasn't around to see this. He'd have told him he had to be firmer with the dog.

Colonel Richardson continued to keep a close eye on Grey over the following week but he'd really already made his decision.

As soon as Nathan saw the colonel heading

towards him and Grey on the training field he quickly jumped to attention.

'At ease, soldier,' Colonel Richardson said.

Grey ran in front of Nathan and then stopped, looked at him and then looked pointedly at his pocket.

'He wants his ball,' Nathan said, and he pulled the ball from his pocket and threw it for Grey to chase after. Grey raced after it and then ran back and dropped it at Nathan's feet.

'You've heard of the parachute regiment?' the colonel asked Nathan.

'Yes, sir.'

'And no doubt you've heard the rumour that there are going to be paradogs?'

Nathan smiled. 'Yes, sir.'

That myth was always going around the War Dog Training School, but Nathan didn't believe it for a minute.

He picked up Grey's ball and threw it for him.

'I'd like you and Grey to give it a try.'

Nathan's eyes opened wide. So the paradog myth was true.

'It'll be dangerous and it's voluntary. Would you be up for it?' the colonel asked.

Nathan thought if any dog could parachute out of a plane, it would be Grey. He wasn't so sure about himself, though – not sure at all.

The colonel was staring at him, waiting for an answer.

'Soldier?'

'Yes, sir,' Nathan said, and with those two words he committed himself and Grey to jumping out of a plane hundreds of feet up in the sky, when in the past he'd always thought twice about riding on the big wheel at a fair.

'Good, you're to report to the paratroop regiment in Manchester in two days' time.'

'Yes, sir.'

'Till then you're on leave.'

'Yes, sir,' Nathan said, smartly. 'Only . . .'

'Yes, soldier?'

'I haven't finished my basic training yet.'

In fact, so far there had been very little basic training and lots of dog-handling training.

'Don't worry – you'll get enough of that and more in the parachute regiment,' the colonel said ruefully.

'Yes, sir,' Nathan said.

'Make the most of your leave,' the colonel told him.

Nathan took a deep breath. 'I'd like to visit my sister during my leave, sir. She's been evacuated to my grandparents' farm in Kent. I wondered if . . .' Nathan hesitated. He was sure he wouldn't be allowed to take Grey away from the War Dog Training School.

'Spit it out, man!'

'Would it be all right for me to take Grey with me?'

Lieutenant Colonel Richardson looked

thoughtful. 'I don't see why not,' he said. 'Don't lose him though. He's too valuable to us.'

'No, sir.'

He was valuable to Nathan too.

'A farm visit could be a useful exercise for him. Don't want him being more terrified of unexpected cattle than Germans when he goes on a reconnaissance mission, do we? Permission granted.'

Nathan couldn't help grinning. 'Thank you, sir.'

Of course Grey might refuse to jump out of a plane, Nathan told himself, as he headed back to the kennels with Grey, and that would be the end of that. He didn't let himself think that he himself might be the one who refused to jump.

Chapter 8

Grey's tail went from wagging to hanging down low when they passed through the doors of Potters Bar train station.

'It's all right,' Nathan said as he stroked the big dog's head.

Grey had learnt so much in the short time they'd been together. Nathan was very proud of him.

'Fine-looking dog,' a man commented as he went past.

No one would call Grey skinny any more, but he was still lean, and very fit.

'There's something almost regal about him,' said one woman with a pheasant feather in her hat.

Nathan looked down at Grey and thought that he did look almost regal, and then realized that the dog now had both ears standing straight up. He didn't know if it was the daily ear-massaging or the regular good food he'd been eating, but Grey's ears were both doing what they were supposed to. Now he looked like an adult German Shepherd. Although Nathan did miss his quirky one-ear-up-and-one-ear-down look a little.

'This way,' Nathan said to Grey when their train arrived. Grey went with him but baulked at the carriage steps. Nathan bent down to help him, but to Nathan's surprise Grey jumped up them instead.

He shook as the whistle blew and the train set off, but soon after that he settled and sat on the floor at Nathan's feet and leant against him.

Nathan noticed that no one wanted to sit near them; he knew many people were frightened of dogs, especially big dogs, and especially Alsatians, as they called them. Nathan stroked Grey's head. In his experience the little dogs were often more of a problem than the big dogs were.

'You wouldn't hurt a fly, would you?' he said.

Penny came running and waving along the platform as soon as she saw Nathan and Grey coming down the carriage steps.

'We've been waiting and waiting for you,' she said as she threw her arms around Grey, who wagged his tail. He was glad to be finally standing on ground that wasn't moving.

'We got here early,' Nathan's grandfather said as he hugged Nathan and patted his back. '*One of us –*' he nodded at Penny – 'kept looking at the clock and worrying about your arrival so much that it was easier just to come to the station.'

'I was so excited I could hardly sleep,' Penny said as she swapped places to hug Nathan while her grandfather said hello to Grey.

'Good-looking dog,' their grandfather said as Grey nuzzled his head into him.

'Best-looking dog in the whole world,' said Penny.

'He's going to be a parachute dog,' Nathan told them.

'A parachute dog!' Penny gasped. 'But dogs can't do that.'

'Yes, they can,' Nathan told her. 'A dog was the first animal to do a parachute jump back in the 1700s.'

'But he doesn't have any hands,' Penny said, practically. 'How's he going to get the parachute off? He can't run around for the rest of the war with a parachute billowing out behind him.' She crouched down and cuddled Grey's furry head.

'No, I'll be parachute jumping too, so I can

release the parachute for him,' Nathan informed them.

'But Nathan,' his grandfather frowned. 'Do you really think that's wise . . . ?'

'How are you going to jump out of a plane when you're too scared even to climb to the top of the tree at the back of the house?' Penny asked him.

Nathan gritted his teeth. 'I'll manage,' he said. Although he certainly wasn't looking forward to it one bit.

'Many men have to do things in war they'd never normally dream of doing in peacetime,' Penny's grandfather told her her, and Nathan nodded, as they all climbed into the farm truck.

'Up, Grey.'

Grey jumped into the truck and lay down on the floor for the short journey.

'Can we show Grey my chickens?' Penny asked, when they got to the farm.

'OK,' Nathan said. 'But we'll have to watch

him carefully. I don't know if he's ever met a chicken before and we don't want him chasing them and making scrambled eggs.'

Penny laughed. 'My chickens won't be frightened,' she said. 'Come on, Grey.'

Nathan followed Penny and his dog over to the chicken run. He was glad the two of them were getting on so well. Maybe Grey had once had a family of his own before he ended up as a stray. He supposed he'd never know where Grey had come from, or exactly what his life had been like, before the war.

As soon as Grey saw the clucking chickens he crouched down low and for an anxious moment Nathan was worried he'd pounce and kill one of them. But then one of the chickens squawked and flapped towards him and Grey turned tail and ran a few feet away.

'It looks like your chickens are safe,' Nathan said as Penny laughed.

'Come on, Grey, they won't hurt you,' Penny

told the dog. But Grey wasn't sure about that and he stayed where he was.

'Grey, come!' Nathan said.

And Grey came to him, his tail between his legs, his eyes looking warily at the feathered creatures. He stopped at Nathan's side and looked round his legs at the chickens, who were much more interested in pecking at the corn Penny scattered for them than in a scaredy dog. Grey spat out the bit of the chicken's corn he'd managed to lick up.

'Let's show him Toffee,' Penny suggested, taking Nathan's hand.

'All right,' Nathan said, although if Grey was scared of chickens he didn't know what he was going to think of the sweet-natured, but huge, shire horse.

Toffee poked her head out of the top of the stable door as they headed towards her and whinnied at the sight of Nathan.

Grey had never seen a horse before and he

wasn't sure about it. It didn't smell like a dog at all.

Toffee had met plenty of dogs, though, when she'd been exhibited at country shows. Most of them had been friendly and a few had been frightened and so not very friendly. She put her head down to blow through her nostrils at Grey and Grey skittered back at first, scared, but then he came forward to sniff her. Toffee blew at him again, her soft breath ruffling his fur.

'Hello, beautiful,' Nathan said as he stroked her and pressed his face into Toffee's neck.

Grey, perhaps responding to the obvious love between Nathan and the horse, wagged his tail. If Nathan wasn't frightened of the strange beast, then neither was he.

When Nathan brought Toffee out of the stable, Grey retreated nervously, but he soon came back as Nathan's voice soothed him.

'It's OK, Grey.'

Grey was very surprised when Nathan swung

himself up on the horse's back. He stayed close to Penny as the Toffee clopped her way round the farmyard.

After his ride, Nathan's gran came hurrying over to envelop him in a hug as they approached the farmhouse. Grey sniffed the air. Nathan's grandmother had been slow-roasting a goose in her oven range since seven o'clock that morning.

Grey had never eaten goose before but the scent of it now made him drool.

'Here you are,' Mrs Dawson said, and she put a plate of roast goose down on the floor for Grey as the rest of the family took their places at the table.

Grey's dish was empty and licked clean almost as soon as Nathan's gran had put it down.

After lunch, Grey got to chase his ball across the farmyard.

'Be careful of my daffodils,' Nathan's gran called out.

'Watch this,' Nathan said to Penny, and he hid Grey's ball in the shed.

'Find it,' Nathan told him, and Grey went into the shed, tail wagging hard, to look for it. He emerged triumphant, with the ball in his mouth, a few moments later.

'He's better at hide and seek than me,' Penny laughed.

'Better than me too,' Nathan grinned.

After dinner, when Grey had goose again, they played blind man's buff and musical chairs, and sang along to 'Mairzy Doats' by the Merry Macs on the radio.

'Mairzy doats and dozy doats and liddle
    lamzy divey
A kiddley divey too, wouldn't you?'

Grey looked up at Nathan and then he looked over at Penny as their voices rang out.

'If the words sound queer and funny to
   your ear, a little bit jumbled and jivey,
Sing: Mares eat oats and does eat oats and
   little lambs eat ivy . . .'

Grey wasn't used to singing and he tried to join
in too, which made everyone laugh. But then
Nathan's gran started crying and Grey went
over to her.

'If only this rotten war could be over,' she
said as she mopped up her tears. Grey laid his
head on her lap and looked up at her.

'You take care of my grandson,' she told Grey.
'Parachute jumping of all things.' She managed
a watery smile and stood up. 'Right, then, who's
ready for some carrot cake? I got the recipe from
the *Home Front Cookery Advice Leaflet.*'

Grey gobbled down a slice of carrot
cake – but for him it couldn't rival the goose
he'd had for lunch and dinner. Nothing
could top that.

Nathan was still asleep when Grey padded out of the room and down the hall the next morning.

'Grey, Grey – come here!' Penny called, as soon as she saw his nose peeping round her bedroom door. She patted her bed cover. 'Grey – come.'

Grey went over to her bed and hopped up on to it, whereupon he was immediately enveloped in a hug and then kissed on the top of his furry head.

'Come and help me feed my chickens.'

Down at the chicken coop Penny threw corn to the birds and Grey tried another bit of corn but spat it out again. Once Penny had collected the eggs, her grandmother made delicious scrambled eggs for them all. Much better. Grey had his with the last of the goose leftovers.

'Don't want you getting hungry on your journey to the parachute regiment,' she said.

'He's a truly good dog,' Nathan's grandfather

said, on their way to the train station. 'You've trained him well.' Grey wagged his tail.

Nathan shook his head. 'Mostly he's trained himself. I just steered him a bit. He's a smart dog.'

Grey saw the train drawing into the station and his tail stopped wagging.

'I'm proud of you, Nathan,' Mr Dawson said as he opened the carriage door for Nathan and Grey to climb on board. This time Grey didn't make a fuss. 'Just make sure you bring that dog and yourself home safe and well.'

Nathan settled Grey as the train set off for Manchester and RAF Ringway. He looked out of the window until he couldn't see his grandfather standing on the platform any more.

Chapter 9

Although he hadn't said so to Penny or his grandparents, Nathan was feeling very worried about parachute jumping, as well as starting at a new camp where he wouldn't know anyone apart from Grey. The War Dog Training School had been designed for dogs and dog handlers, whereas the airbase was designed for the Army Air Corps. He hadn't even properly finished his basic training and now it looked like he was going to be a paratrooper, as long as he passed, alongside some of the fittest soldiers there were.

So he was more than a little nervous as he and Grey were checked in at the gate.

'I thought it was a joke when they said we might be getting a trainee paradog,' the guard told Nathan.

'No joke,' Nathan said.

'Crazy,' the guard muttered.

Grey wagged his tail.

Nathan could feel the guard's eyes watching him and Grey as they walked into the camp. It made him feel uncomfortable but it didn't seem to bother Grey at all.

As the dog strolled confidently by his side through the camp, Nathan found it hard to remember him as a stray dog, and he certainly didn't look like one any more. He looked like a proud military dog, especially now both his ears were standing up straight. But whether he could be a paradog remained to be seen.

A squad of soldiers jogged past and some of them stared at Grey.

'Eyes front, soldiers,' the sergeant shouted at them.

'Come on, Grey,' Nathan said, and Grey looked up at him and wagged his tail at the sound of his name.

Grey was used to there being lots of other dogs about at the War Dog Training School, but here there were no sounds of barking or scents of different dogs in the air. Here he was the only dog, although other dogs were being trained to parachute jump at other air bases. Nathan wasn't sure why Grey and he couldn't be trained with those other dogs and their handlers, but he was a soldier and his job was to obey orders without question, so that's what he intended to do.

At least there was a brand-new kennel waiting for Grey.

Grey sniffed at it and detected that the kennel had had a visit from a mouse earlier in the day. Grey was very fond of mice and the smell reminded him of happy times with Molly in the shed back in Dover, when they would hunt for mice together.

'Welcome to your new home,' Nathan said as he clipped Grey's lead to the kennel and went to find his commanding officer. Grey barked as he left, but Nathan didn't turn back. Grey barked again and then he whined, but Nathan was gone. So Grey had a long drink of cool water from the bowl beside his kennel and then lay down to wait for his friend to come back. He was getting more and more used to Nathan leaving him, and gradually learning to trust that he would come back for him.

'You've heard about the Calais mission?' Nathan's commanding officer, Major Parry, asked him.

'Yes, sir,' Nathan said.

'Well, as Calais is the closest port to your hometown of Dover, you'll know all about the

Germans' efforts to attack it with the large cannon-like guns they've aimed squarely at it,' Major Parry explained.

'Yes, sir. I'm very much looking forward to the day those guns finally stop firing.'

'Well, the real story is that the Calais mission is just a decoy mission and not really going to happen,' the major said.

Nathan's eyes widened in surprise.

'It's a trick to deceive the German military chiefs,' the major continued.

Nathan thought the trick had worked very well so far. Everyone was talking about the Pas-de-Calais mission. It seemed the only logical area for the Allied forces to strike, especially as it was so close to Britain.

'The real mission is going to take place further round the coast, along the beaches of Normandy. We're looking for men like you, and your dog, to undertake reconnaissance missions and report back on what guns and other munitions the Germans have in Normandy, right up until the moment we attack.'

'Yes, sir,' Nathan said.

'It'll be extremely dangerous and if you're caught . . .' The major looked down at the papers on the table in front of him. 'Well, just don't get caught.'

Nathan gulped. 'No, sir.'

'You'll need extra language and code lessons.'

'Yes, sir.'

'And your dog will need extra infantry training as well as parachute training. It's a lot to ask.'

'We won't let you down, sir,' Nathan said.

'Keep all this under your hat,' the major told him. 'Everything I've told you today is to be kept top secret. Hitler needs to keep thinking our intended landing area is Calais until it's too late.'

Nathan left the major's office feeling slightly dazed but very excited too.

He headed back to Grey's kennel only to find that the dog was no longer alone. There was a black and white cat sitting on the kennel roof.

'Don't mind Astor,' a smiling man told him, as he came over with a bone for Grey. 'She loves dogs and she's a great mouser. My name's Bert, by the way. I'm the camp's chef. Pleased to meet you.'

After supper Nathan took Grey for a walk round the grounds and found that although there weren't any other dogs, Grey wasn't the only animal at the camp. Over on the opposite side pigeons were being trained to be messengers. There were chickens that laid eggs for the soldiers' breakfasts and pigs that ate the food from the pig bins brought in on the back of a truck once a week. The chickens and pigs were kept in a field at the furthest edge of the camp and that's where Billy, the camp's goat mascot, or lucky charm, lived too.

As soon as Billy saw Grey he came running across the field to him and the two animals touched noses through the fence. Grey had never seen a goat before and was very interested in this strange creature.

After Nathan had settled him in and left him for the night, Grey was lonely in his solitary kennel until Billy came to join him.

Billy was supposed to stay in the pig field when he wasn't being a mascot, but he wasn't the sort of goat that ever did what he was supposed to do. Billy was the sort of goat who did just exactly what he liked.

Late at night he trotted over to Grey's kennel where he found the dog lying outside his kennel, although still chained to it, not asleep but dozing lightly.

Grey stood up and wagged his tail, a little

unsure. Billy came closer and let Grey sniff at him. Then he went over to Grey's food bowl to see if he'd left anything in it, which of course he hadn't. Both Grey and Billy had large appetites.

Billy turned and trotted off and Grey tried to follow him but couldn't because of the chain. He barked to let Billy know he was stuck and the goat turned back and made a bleating sound before heading off again.

Grey had never tried to escape from his collar and chain before, but now he found that if he pulled his head backwards, like a tortoise going into its shell, he was able to squeeze his way out of it. Once free, he ran to catch up with Billy and the two of them explored the camp together before being joined by the cook's cat, Astor, on her nightly mouse hunt.

Just before dawn Billy returned to his field, Astor went home to the kitchen and Grey crept back to his kennel.

While the animals prowled the camp, Nathan stared up at the bunk above his own and listened to the sounds of other soldiers snoring and muttering in their sleep. He worried that he'd made a terrible mistake in agreeing to come here and if he were truly honest he was completely terrified of having to jump out of a plane. Just the thought of it made him feel sick. He wished he'd said no, but he felt he hadn't really had a choice when Lieutenant Colonel Richardson asked him, and he really didn't want to let the colonel down. He was far more worried about jumping from the plane than going on an undercover mission once he'd landed.

As soon as the reveille sounded at 6.30 a.m., Nathan headed over to check on Grey, but as he approached he saw two uniformed men standing in front of Grey's kennel. They seemed to be shouting at him. Nathan started running towards them.

'*Sitzen, hund!*' yelled one of the men, who wore a pilot's uniform.

'*Stehan!*' shrieked the other, who had on Army Air Corps kit.

Grey watched the men attentively, his head tilted to one side and then the other. He didn't look like he was even on his lead. They must have released his collar.

'*Sprechen sie Deutsch, Hund?*'

Nathan came running over.

'Hey, what are you doing?' he yelled. 'Leave my dog alone. Why've you removed his collar? He could have run off.'

'We didn't take his collar off.'

'He wasn't wearing it when we got here.'

Nathan didn't believe them for a minute. 'I suppose he took it off himself, did he?' he muttered as he put a tail-wagging Grey's collar back on him.

'Didn't you hear?' the pilot, whose name was Tommy, said.

'Hear what?' Nathan asked him.

'Your dog might be able to speak.'

Nathan clenched his fists.

'What on earth are you talking about?' he said. The two men were a lot bigger than him, but he wouldn't let them intimidate him and he wouldn't let them hurt Grey.

'Hitler's got a dog school that's teaching dogs to talk.'

'Here, look.' The pilot pulled a crumpled newspaper clipping from his pocket and handed it to Nathan. It was about a place called the Asra Talking School for Dogs, based near Hanover in Germany. The Nazis were sponsoring research into whether dogs could actually speak, and the article claimed that dogs were being trained to talk and count at the school.

'So Hitler really is trying to get dogs to talk,' Nathan said, and he shook his head in disbelief. The men weren't joking. He gave the pilot his newspaper cutting back and looked into Grey's blue eyes. If dogs could talk he was sure Grey would be able to. But then he decided Grey didn't need to speak because one look or movement from his eyes or a tilt of his head was enough to tell Nathan exactly what he wanted.

'Successfully teaching a dog to speak is about as likely as being able to teach one to jump out of a plane,' Gordon, the other soldier, laughed.

'It's been done before, actually,' Nathan told him. 'Grey won't be the first paradog by a long shot.'

'Well, I won't believe it until I've seen it with my own eyes,' Gordon said.

'Let's be honest – it's hard enough for a soldier to jump out of a plane, and I should know because I fly the planes they go up in, so I can't imagine it would be any easier for a dog,' Tommy told him.

Nathan half agreed with Tommy but what he said was, 'If any dog can do it, Grey can. He's going to help our soldiers and save lots of

lives – maybe even your life; maybe even mine.'
His heart swelled with pride at the very thought
of it.

Muttering apologies, Tommy and Gordon
sloped off to the mess hall and it was time for
Grey's breakfast.

The parachute regiment didn't have any dog
food yet but Grey certainly didn't mind when
Nathan came back with food that Bert the cook
had given him. Eggs and bacon with sausages,
black pudding and potatoes for breakfast was
just fine by Grey.

'You are one lucky dog,' Nathan told him as
he watched him eating.

The dog had become such a big part of his
life now that it was hard to remember what life
had been like before he knew him. How on
earth had he managed without a dog before?
He couldn't imagine life without one now.

Grey had almost finished his breakfast when
he started wagging his tail.

'What's going on?' Nathan asked, as the dog gulped down the last bit of black pudding.

He looked over and saw the regimental goat being led along by the Goat Major on a lead. It bleated as it trotted past Grey.

'Meh-eh-eh!'

Nathan grinned as Grey's tail carried on wagging. 'Already making friends, I see,' he said.

Chapter 10

The men and dogs of the parachute regiment needed to be exceptionally fit, and daily three-mile runs, which Grey came on too, were the norm come rain or shine.

Nathan hadn't had nearly as much physical training as the other men and was also a lot younger and slighter than them. Although he did his best, he usually ended up at the back.

'Come on, you slow coaches,' Sergeant Harris shouted at the running soldiers. 'This dog can run twice as fast as you lot.'

Nathan thought that was probably – no

definitely – true. He gritted his teeth and kept running while he watched Grey wagging his tail as he raced to the men at the front and then back to join Nathan. The dog easily ran twice as far as the rest of them and yet didn't seem to be half as tired at the end of the run.

It was a breezy morning and Nathan had a nervous feeling in the pit of his stomach as he stood with the other soldiers on the jump practice field.

'It's no good doing a perfect jump if you don't land right,' the sergeant told the men and Grey. 'Far more of you are going to be injured on landing than at any other time during your jump. So the first thing you'll have to learn is how to land safely.'

A crash mat had been placed next to a six-foot block and each of the trainee paratroopers had to jump from it in turn.

'Keep your knees bent,' the sergeant told the first soldier as he jumped off the block. 'When you come down for real you want to keep your legs up so they don't get broken.'

The soldier rolled off the mat and Sergeant Harris nodded to Nathan.

'You next.'

Nathan gave Grey's lead to the soldier standing beside him to hold and ignored the dog's whine of protest. Nathan found even climbing up the block difficult because of his fear of heights.

'Get a move on, soldier!' Sergeant Harris shouted.

Nathan clenched his fists determinedly.

'Go!'

Nathan closed his eyes, jumped and rolled on to the crash mat as Grey broke free from the soldier who was holding him and raced to Nathan's side.

'That's how it should be done,' the sergeant

said as Grey gave Nathan's face a lick. Nathan stood up and went to join the rest of the men with Grey sticking close by his side. But although Nathan might have been able to land correctly it didn't mean he wanted to do it again. He was dreading the next stage of the training. The distance he would have to jump was going to be a lot bigger very soon.

In the afternoon everyone was issued with their parachute kits from the quartermaster's stores. Nathan took Grey with him.

Because the soldiers weighed a lot more than the dogs, the canine parachutists needed different parachutes from the humans.

'Bicycle parachute for the dog,' the quarter-master said, handing Grey's parachute to Nathan.

'Bicycle parachute?' Nathan asked.

'Your dog weighs about the same as an errand-boy's bike,' the quartermaster explained to him. 'So we're giving him the same sort of parachute as we put on the bicycles we're dropping into France – so you lot can blend in with the locals if you need to go undercover. Can't just throw the bicycles down from the planes, can we? They need to land gently if they're going to work properly.'

Nathan secured the buckles of Grey's parachute harness as tightly as they would go without hurting him. The straps went over Grey's back and under his tummy to circle him securely and then round the back of his legs. The kit needed to be tight so it wouldn't slip, and was exactly the right size. A harness that moved while Grey was jumping out of the plane could affect how the parachute performed and be fatal.

The soldiers also wore secure parachute harnesses. They were able to put their own on but were always checked by another soldier to make sure they were correctly fitted and had been put on properly. As well as the harness and parachute, Nathan had a camouflage smock, a life jacket and a first-aid kit.

'Are there life jackets for dogs?' Nathan asked, but was told that the life jackets the soldiers were wearing, jokingly referred to as Mae Wests, weren't suitable for dogs.

'He's not going to be landing in the sea; they're just a precaution,' the quartermaster reassured him.

'Do we really have to wear all this while we're practising,' Gordon muttered, and Sergeant Harris heard him.

'Yes you do, soldier, yes you do. Those parachutes have got to become as much a part of you as its shell is to a tortoise. Understand?'

'Yes, sir,' Gordon said.

Sergeant Harris divided the soldiers into three squads: A, B and C. Nathan and Grey were in A squad.

'Let's see if you lot can manage to jump from

a plane that's got its engine off and is down on the ground,' Sergeant Harris said. 'A squad, line up.'

Grey and Nathan stood with the other soldiers from their squad in a line outside the rear door of the plane. It had no steps up to the door and Nathan knew Grey wouldn't be able to climb the narrow bar ladder. Grey looked up at him. The tension in Nathan's body had transferred down his lead again and he knew something was wrong. He whined.

'It's OK, Grey, good dog,' Nathan said, trying to reassure Grey and himself at the same time.

'Ready, soldier?' Sergeant Harris said.

'Yes, sir,' Nathan lied. The very thought of climbing the ladder made his head swim, and his knees were feeling very wobbly indeed.

The only one who knew how awful he truly felt was Grey, and Nathan tried hard not to let his own fear affect the dog's performance. Grey was doing so well that Nathan owed it to him to keep going. He couldn't let him down.

'I'll pass your dog up to you, soldier,' Sergeant Harris said.

'Thank you, sir,' Nathan replied.

He climbed up the thin metal ladder and waited at the plane's doorway for Grey.

Sergeant Harris bent to pick up Grey but before he could get a grip on him Grey struggled up the awkward ladder all by himself and into the plane after Nathan.

'Good dog. Carry on,' the sergeant said.

There were no seats inside the plane and the men and Grey sat on the floor, against the sides. Along the centre was a thick wire for the jumpers to hook their parachute clips to. They then waited for the pilot to let them know when it was safe to jump. Nathan would clip Grey's on for him, but because today was their first day of training the plane wasn't actually going to leave the ground and so the central wire wasn't being used.

'You first, soldier,' Sergeant Harris told Nathan.

Nathan swallowed hard and dug his fingernails into the palms of his hands. He went with Grey to stand at the exit door and tried not to look down, but couldn't help it. The plane hadn't even left the tarmac, the engine wasn't running and the plane was perfectly still, but nevertheless he really didn't want to jump out.

Nathan tried to steady his breath as he checked Grey's parachute. He felt as if he was going to faint, but he knew he couldn't.

'On the green light,' Sergeant Harris said.

Nathan looked at the red light that turned to green. He took a deep breath.

'Go green!'

Nathan closed his eyes as he stepped out of the plane into thin air. As he fell he tucked himself into a ball and rolled on to a mat on the ground to reduce the landing impact.

'Come, Grey!' Nathan yelled, and Grey immediately leapt out of the stationary plane after him. Nathan grabbed his collar and they ran out of the way as the next trainee paratrooper jumped from the plane.

Grey enthusiastically licked Nathan's face.

'Yes, you're a good dog, a very good dog, a very clever dog!' Nathan told him as Grey wagged his tail and hopped around him.

Nathan was dreading having to do it again.

'That was great, wasn't it?' the trainee paratroopers said as they slapped each other on the back and congratulated themselves once they'd all jumped.

'Can't wait to try something higher.'

'Looking forward to doing it for real.'

Nathan nodded, although he didn't really agree at all. He wasn't looking forward to going any higher or doing a 'real' parachute jump.

'Your dog's amazing,' Gordon told him.

'You'd think he'd been parachute jumping all his life.'

'Doesn't seem to have an ounce of fear about jumping out of a plane,' someone else said.

And Nathan smiled because he did agree with them about that. Grey was truly one totally amazing dog. As Nathan headed back to the kennels with Grey later that day he looked back at the plane. It was almost impossible to believe that he'd actually jumped out of it. He shook his head and looked down at Grey who wagged his tail. If it hadn't been for the dog, he'd never have managed it.

As frightening as the prospect of more real parachute jumping from a flying plane was, he'd rather do it a hundred times than lose the chance to work with Grey.

Chapter 11

Nathan struggled with his extra language and code lessons before their mission, but Grey revelled in his extra agility classes and messenger-dog training. The messenger-dog collar was hollow so that messages could be put inside it, lightweight and made of strong leather. Usually messenger dogs only wore them when they were taking messages, but on Nathan and Grey's mission to France he'd wear it all the time as there wasn't room to take extra collars.

Part of Grey's training involving searching

for Nathan. He was held while Nathan hid, and as soon as he was released he raced to find him. The distances over which Grey had to look for Nathan were increased and increased.

When he did find him there was always lots of praise, something nice to eat as reward, followed by a game of ball – his favourite activity.

Sergeant Harris was very impressed and so were the other soldiers when they heard about it. They came to watch as Grey was released and went to find Nathan.

'He'll never find him this time . . .'

'I bet he will . . .'

'You've never seen anything like this . . .'

Nathan moved from hiding place to hiding place while Grey was looking for him so he'd leave a trail of scents but the dog always found him. Grey was taken to different locations and in a forest had to jump over fallen branches and cross a small stream before he found Nathan. But still he found him.

'That dog is really something, you know,' Gordon told Nathan back at the barracks. He had his hands in his pockets and was looking down at his feet. Nathan thought he was probably embarrassed about the day he'd caught him shouting in German outside Grey's kennel.

'Just got to teach him to speak German now,' Nathan grinned, and Gordon looked up with relief and grinned back.

'Look at that!' the soldiers said the next morning as Sergeant Harris led them all over to the training field, wearing their parachute gear. In front of them a huge grey barrage balloon, nearly thirty feet long, floated 600 feet up in the sky.

Grey had seen lots of barrage balloons before in Dover. They had been up in the sky ever since he was a puppy and he wasn't the least bit fazed by this one.

'Right, you lot,' Sergeant Harris said. 'We'll be jumping from that balloon today. It isn't as far up as a plane will be and it doesn't move as fast.'

The balloon had a box-like cage beneath it and was attached to a lorry with a winch on the back.

'You three and the dog first,' the sergeant said.

Nathan, Grey and two other soldiers headed over to the balloon and the lorry winch brought it down so they could climb into the cage.

'All right, my lovelies,' said the Women's Auxiliary Air Force officer who was in charge of the balloon, and she winched them up.

Once they were high in the sky, Nathan again pressed his fingernails hard into the palms of his hands to steady himself.

'The first parachute dog floated down from a hot-air balloon in the 1700s,' Nathan told the others, to distract himself from his nerves. But none of them were really paying any attention and they all looked very nervous. Only Grey was blissfully unaware of what was about to happen.

'That's it, Grey, you'll be fine,' Nathan told the dog, who looked at him with trust in his clear blue eyes.

Nathan felt bad because he didn't know if he and Grey were really going to be all right or not. Looking down from 600 feet up only made him feel more queasy. It was such a long way down.

'You first, then I'll send down the dog,' Sergeant Harris said.

Nathan just nodded because he couldn't trust himself to speak.

'Go!'

As he stepped through the gap into air, Nathan closed his eyes and for a moment he wanted to scream, but then the parachute opened and his descent became much slower as he floated gently down to the ground.

Above him, Grey was floating down too and he could hear the dog barking. It wasn't a frightened-sounding bark, though – it was one of excitement. Grey sounded like he was having the time of his life. And Nathan started to laugh. He laughed and laughed, and with his laughter his terrible fear of heights, that had been a part of his life for so long, disappeared into thin air.

Parachute jumping was exhilarating and it made him feel more alive than he'd ever felt before. He would refuse to let himself ever feel frightened of heights again and he was looking forward to future jumps with his incredible dog.

'Good dog,' Nathan said as he released his own parachute and then ran over to release Grey's. Grey wagged his tail enthusiastically and gave Nathan's face a big lick.

Back at the barracks, Nathan slapped a pasty-looking Gordon on the back.

'That was great, wasn't it?' he grinned.

'Well, you and the dog certainly seemed to like it,' Gordon said. 'Personally from now on I'd like to keep both feet firmly on the ground.'

Nathan laughed and went to fetch Grey's dinner before the evening's scheduled first-aid class. The trainee paratroopers needed to know what to do if they or their fellow soldiers were injured in the field. Nathan was also taught how to help Grey if he were hurt.

While Nathan attended his class, Grey and Astor rested close to Grey's kennel until Bert came over to them.

'Hungry?' he asked, and he gave a large ham bone to Grey and some just-cooked ham to Astor. Once the camp had settled down for the night they were joined by Billy, but once again, when morning came Grey was alone.

'I don't understand how your collar keeps coming off at night,' Nathan said as he rebuckled it round Grey's neck.

Grey wagged his tail and licked Nathan's hand, ready for another day full of adventures.

The dog still showed no fear of heights and loved running along the narrow beam and the A-frame during the extra agility lessons he went to straight after his morning run with the rest of the soldiers. Soon word got round the men about how good at it he was and they came out to watch him as he completed the course and then they all cheered him at the end of it.

They watched as Grey crawled on his belly through a narrow pipe too small for a man to squeeze through to find Nathan and a treat waiting for him.

'Good dog, Grey,' Nathan told him. 'Good dog.'

Grey kept looking over at the tunnel he'd

come through, obviously excited and ready to do more.

'Let's try him on the split tunnel,' Sergeant Harris suggested.

'Sit, Grey, stay,' Nathan told the dog.

Grey sat and waited as Nathan walked away from him to the other end of the split tunnel.

'Grey, come!' Nathan called and Grey ran into the narrow tunnel, which split into two.

'Come,' Nathan called again, and Grey squeezed his way into the narrower of the dark tunnels, crawled along it on his belly and pushed open a flap at the end to find Nathan, whose face he promptly licked as Nathan laughed while the rest of the men cheered.

'Fifteen seconds,' Sergeant Harris said, looking at his stopwatch as the men applauded.

Grey was very fast for such a large dog. Best of all, he didn't need to be told over and over what he needed to do; he picked it up in no time and often correctly guessed what Nathan wanted him to do even before he'd asked him to do it.

A few days later Nathan fixed the bicycle parachute harness around Grey's body.

'Final training jump today,' he told the dog. They'd made seven jumps so far; three from the balloons and four from planes.

Grey wagged his tail and then jumped confidently up into the plane. The routine never varied and the commands and positions were always the same. That way, in a panic situation, the men would know what to do without needing to think. Each paratrooper checked the harness of the man in front of him and Nathan checked Grey's.

Sergeant Harris shouted, 'Fit equipment,' which meant it was time for Nathan to attach the parachute to the harness in the middle of Grey's back. It was heavy for a dog to carry. Too heavy really, in Nathan's opinion. But once Grey was out of the plane and flying through the air he wouldn't notice the parachute's weight, and if it had been too light it wouldn't have the support or strength it needed and the dog would end up being tossed around in the wind.

'Sound off for equipment check,' Sergeant Harris shouted above the noise of the plane as it made its ascent. 'One OK, two OK, three OK . . .' came the reply from each of the men. Everyone kept exactly to the script.

Once everyone had called out their reply, Sergeant Harris shouted, 'Hook up.'

Nathan clipped the hook from Grey's parachute bag to the plane's central wire. Then he attached his own parachute hook to it and everyone else who was going to jump from the plane did exactly the same.

The light by the plane's door was red and they had to wait for it to turn green before anyone could jump. The pilot and co-pilot controlled the light switch and they would only give the parachutists the go-ahead once they were at a steady speed and it was as safe as it could be for the men to jump. They reached 600 feet.

'Red on . . .' Sergeant Harris shouted.

The wind was strong and the plane was juddery as it flew up to a height of 800 feet. But it still didn't seem to worry Grey. He wagged his tail as Nathan rechecked that his harness was secure.

The green light came on.

'Green on . . . Go,' Sergeant Harris said to Nathan.

Nathan jumped out of the plane and a few seconds later Grey came after him. Nathan could at least hold on to the strings of his parachute, but Grey couldn't. He had no way of controlling his parachute and was totally dependent on Nathan to release him from it once they hit the ground.

As soon as he landed, Nathan released his own parachute and looked up at Grey coming down. The dog's landing was perfect and Nathan ran over to unstrap him from his kit.

'We did it,' he told Grey, who wagged his tail and licked his face, bounding in a circle around him, exuberantly.

That evening there was a graduation ceremony and Nathan took Grey to the front of the room with him when he and the other soldiers in his squad were given their coveted red berets and winged badges.

Grey wasn't given a beret, of course, but Nathan gave him something even better – a shiny new red ball. Grey happily chewed on it while Nathan wrote to Penny and his mother to tell them that he was now officially a paratrooper and Grey a paradog.

He'd only just finished writing the letter when Major Parry's aide came to find him.

It was time for Nathan and Grey's mission to France to begin.

Chapter 12

It was very late at night but Grey was instantly awake and wagging his tail as soon as Nathan stopped at his kennel.

'Time to go,' Nathan said.

Grey didn't know where they were going. All that mattered was that he was going with Nathan.

'There'll be no nice kennel for you once we're in Normandy, my friend,' Nathan told Grey. 'And probably just a dug-out hole for us both to sleep in, if we're lucky.'

Nathan clipped Grey's lead to his collar and they headed over to the waiting bomber plane.

'Up, Grey,' Nathan said. But Grey didn't jump up as he usually did. He stayed where he was, then looked up at Nathan and whined, his tail between his legs. 'Come on now, you like going in planes,' Nathan encouraged him. But Grey only tried to pull Nathan away too. 'No,' Nathan told him firmly and Grey stopped pulling. 'Good dog,' Nathan said.

He didn't blame Grey for his momentary terror at all. He didn't want to get on the bomber either, but this was war and their mission was vital; neither he nor Grey had a choice. They had to do their job. Thousands of soldiers would be arriving on the Normandy beaches in the next few weeks and before they got there they needed to know what guns the German army had so they didn't walk into an ambush.

'Up, Grey – go on,' Nathan said. And when Grey again refused to board Nathan picked him up and put him on the plane. 'Sorry, but it had to be done,' Nathan told him, as Grey gave him a look and whined.

'Does that dog need a muzzle?' Tommy the pilot shouted from the cockpit.

'No, he'll be fine,' Nathan shouted back. A muzzle would only make things worse.

'You sure? A crazed dog's teeth biting us isn't going to help anyone. A bandage wrapped round his mouth will keep us – and him – safe.'

'He'll be fine,' Nathan repeated firmly.

Tommy hesitated. He may well need the bandages they'd been issued with to treat an injury.

'Sure as sure?'

'Absolutely, he's always been perfectly fine in planes before and ready and eager to jump out – just got a bit of stage fright, that's all.'

Nathan breathed a sigh of relief as Tommy nodded and turned back to his instruments. He stroked Grey's furry head.

The dog was much less happy about being in the bomber than Nathan had ever seen him before. As the engines started and the plane juddered, Grey was shaking. He looked utterly miserable – even more unhappy than when he'd travelled on the train for the first time.

As the plane took off, Astor watched it from the top of Grey's kennel and Billy watched from his field.

The steep rise caused a painful pressure in Nathan's ears.

'Blow hard while holding your nose,' Tommy shouted over his shoulder. Nathan did so but poor Grey couldn't.

The plane flying Nathan and Grey to France banked low over the training camp, then levelled off and flew up into the night sky.

The atmosphere on board wasn't at all like it had been on the training missions. It was much more intense. Nathan tried to stay calm for Grey's sake, knowing how the dog picked up on his emotions, but he only just managed to keep his queasiness under control as the plane flew onwards.

At their final briefing before the mission, Major Parry had told them that members of the Resistance would be waiting for them, ready to show them the Germans' latest guns. Nathan tried to focus his thoughts on the importance of locating these brave fighters and how he mustn't let them down. The information they'd be waiting to pass on would be crucial to the war effort.

The cloudy sky was perfect for their undercover mission, but, although visibility was low, the worst happened and they were spotted.

Nathan didn't hear the sound of the second plane above the noise of their own plane's engine, but Grey did.

'We've got company,' Tommy shouted as the German plane came closer.

They'd hoped to fly into France undetected, but soon Nathan and Tommy started to hear the unmistakeable sound of *ack-ack* as anti-aircraft fire shot into the air around them. If they took a direct hit, Grey and Nathan and Tommy would be killed – unless they could get out in time. There was no way Nathan was going to allow himself or Grey to die trapped inside a flying metal coffin. They'd jump out right now if they had to.

'Hang on, I might be able to outmanoeuvre him,' Tommy said. He swerved and dipped as he tried to escape the other plane's guns but the Germans stayed firmly on their tail and shot at them. 'Incoming from the right,' Tommy shouted as a second German plane hurtled up to join the first. He might have had a chance of taking on the plane, but tackling two was impossible.

'Prepare to bail out!' he shouted to Nathan. Nathan stood up and checked that Grey's parachute harness was secure one last time. Even in the panic of the situation they were in, the hours of training paid off.

'Now!'

Nathan pushed an unwilling Grey out of the plane and then jumped himself. His descent was through the clouds; he was cold and wet and almost undetectable from the ground because of the rainy sky.

He couldn't see Grey or Tommy as he floated down and he knew they could be miles away. The high wind and lashing rain as well as the chaotic circumstances of their jump as they tried to evade the other planes' guns meant there was virtually no chance of them landing anywhere near each other. But still Nathan hoped against hope that Grey would be somewhere close by and unhurt.

His parachute landing was soft because of the early summer floods and he jumped to his feet, unclipped his chute, tore it off and stuffed it in a bush to hide it as quickly as possible. Then he looked around for Grey. It was very dark and he could barely see anything because of the lashing rain. He made a whistling sound through his teeth. He couldn't call out in case he alerted the enemy, but there was no response to his whistle and, as Nathan waded knee deep through the flooded fields, he felt sick with dread.

The army had prepared them all as well as it could, but one of the things Nathan's group of soldiers hadn't been taught how to do was swim.

He whistled quietly again as he circled the area, hoping for an answering bark or a whine or anything at all, but there was nothing – just a terrible silence.

Grey didn't have a life jacket. They weren't designed for dogs to wear and Nathan didn't know whether Grey could swim or not. He'd been told that dogs can swim instinctively, but he didn't know if this was really always true or not.

If only he'd taken Grey swimming. If only he could be sure. But it was too late now.

Then an even worse thought came to him. Even if Grey could swim he wouldn't be able to get out of his parachute. He needed someone to remove it, and that person should have been Nathan.

'Grey,' Nathan called out. 'Grey!'

As if from nowhere, a hand appeared and clamped itself over his mouth.

'Shut up! Or we'll all be killed,' a voice with a French accent ordered him.

It was a member of the French Resistance who had been waiting for them, as planned. The man released his hand from Nathan's mouth.

'My dog,' Nathan whispered. 'We parachuted together . . .'

The man had never met Nathan or Grey

and so Nathan knew he couldn't possibly begin to understand the bond he and the dog had.

'I have seen no dog,' he muttered. 'And there's no time to look for it now. Come on!'

The man pushed him roughly forward and Nathan knew he had no choice but to go. He needed to report back about the guns; his comrades at home were counting on him. The man from the French Resistance introduced himself as Jacques Dubois, and he and Nathan waded on through the flooded field.

'They've brought more guns – big guns,' Jacques told him as they reached the edge of the field where Nathan saw that he had a motorcycle waiting for them. He pulled away the tree branches he'd used to hide it. 'They took them to the Merville gun battery. I will show you.'

He climbed on to his motorcycle and, after one last desperate look behind him to see if Grey was there, Nathan climbed on too.

Jacques started the engine and they drove – without headlights so it would be harder for the enemy to spot them – towards the German gun battery. All the time Nathan prayed that Grey was all right; that he wouldn't be caught; that wherever he'd landed someone would help him remove the parachute that he couldn't remove for himself.

He felt desperately guilty as he imagined Grey lying injured and afraid. Had he landed safely somewhere? Often parachutists landed in trees and were stuck there unless they managed to cut themselves free. But Grey didn't have a knife or hands that could grip one. He was solely dependent on someone to release his parachute for him.

For a moment Nathan wondered if it would have been better for Grey if they had never met. Nathan felt it certainly wouldn't have been better for himself, but if Nathan hadn't rescued him Grey could have gone back to life as a stray dog in Dover. It had been a tough life admittedly, but maybe better than being lost in France.

'*Voila*,' Jacques said as the motorcycle stopped. 'From here we walk.'

Nathan helped Jacques to hide his motorcycle under more foliage and they set off to trudge through the rain for the last mile towards the Germans' gun enplacement. It was well protected not only with barbed wire, but also by a minefield through which Jacques led Nathan carefully.

'Over there,' he said as he handed Nathan a pair of wire-cutters to cut through the barbed wire. The huge gun fort, made of concrete and steel to protect the guns within, lay just ahead. It was hard to see exactly what was inside the fort, but there were holes in it for the largest of the guns to poke through. The guns could do devastating damage to the Allied forces and the British needed to know about them as soon as possible.

But Nathan wanted to see more so that he would have more intelligence to report. They crept closer and were just inside it when they were almost spotted.

'*Wer ist das?*' a voice asked.

Nathan and Jaques ran to hide as footsteps approached.

'Miau, is that you?' the German soldier said. He stopped in front of the large cannon-shaped gun behind which Nathan was hiding.

Nathan held his breath as a cat miaowed and came running to the soldier.

'Aha, was it you catching mice again?' the soldier said as he lifted the cat into his arms. 'Let's see if we can find you some milk, little Miau.'

As soon as the German soldier had gone, Nathan and Jaques ran. They made it safely out of the gun battery, but as they were running through the minefield a shot rang out.

'My leg,' yelled Jacques. 'I've been hit!'

Then, 'Go, go, go!' he shouted, as Nathan instinctively went to help him.

'No!' Jacques begged, holding up his hand as Nathan knelt beside him. 'Too risky to save me. Tell them there is also a railway gun . . .'

Nathan pulled Jacques's arm round him and dragged him to his feet.

'You must report what you see. If you do not, all this will be a waste,' Jacques begged.

But there was no way Nathan would leave Jacques to be taken prisoner or maybe even shot.

'They need the railway-gun information too,' he said, through gritted teeth, as he half dragged the much heavier man away through the torrential rain. Although the rain was drenching both of them to the skin, it would at least make them harder to see.

Chapter 13

The flooded river's current was so strong that Grey had no chance of swimming against it, and with the parachute still attached and no way for him to remove it, he was in very grave danger of drowning.

He tried and tried to reach the bank, but the rushing river refused to let him. The parachute weighed him down and finally he was too exhausted to fight the river any more. He stopped trying and let the rushing water carry him away, his head sinking under the water as he was pulled down.

Suddenly, however, he was stopped by a sharp jolt. The parachute strings had caught on the branch of a fallen tree, which stopped his progress down the river. Grey was able to half clamber on to the tree and cling there. All night he held on, shivering and wet. All night he waited for Nathan to find him.

By the time the sun rose Grey was half delirious. He was so cold and so tired and so lost without Nathan. He slipped in and out of consciousness, and when he finally did hear voices they seemed to be coming from very far away.

'*Un chien!*' Claude cried, pointing at the dog in the river.

He and Sabine ran towards it, but as she ran Sabine was worried the dog would be dead, and she couldn't bear for this war to take any more lives.

'Be careful,' Claude begged her as Sabine

crawled out along the branch of the tree and found herself staring into a pair of terrified blue eyes.

'It's all right,' she said softly. 'It's all right. I'm going to set you free.'

The dog was so weak she had to be careful the current didn't drag him away once the parachute that was trapping and also supporting him was released.

'Get Luc,' she shouted to her brother. 'And then run home and bring the cart.' The dog didn't look strong enough to walk and he'd be too heavy for them to carry home.

Luc's family was part of the French Resistance too.

Sabine was frightened for Luc and Claude, and for herself, but she knew, also, that they had to help the Allies if France was ever to regain its freedom.

Luc was fourteen and lived on the farm next to theirs. He was very quiet and shy – sometimes he barely said a word all day – but he was also very strong and Sabine was glad when he came running to help.

As she carefully unravelled the parachute strings she gave them to Luc to hold on to so that if the dog were dragged away by the current he'd be able to pull him back.

Claude ran up, breathless, pulling the hand cart, but it wasn't needed. Luc cradled the dog in his arms, holding Grey close to him to keep him warm. Grey shivered with shock, cold and exhaustion as Luc told him he would be safe now. He couldn't understand the boy's words, but he knew the tone of Luc's voice meant comfort and security, warmth and love.

Luc carried Grey all the way back to Sabine and Claude's farmhouse and laid him gently on a blanket in front of the fire while Claude ran to fetch more sticks to build up the flames. Sabine knelt beside the dog and stroked him.

They were still kneeling beside Grey when

Sabine and Claude's mother came back from the market.

She gasped when she saw the large dog lying fast asleep in front of the fireplace. Grey was the first dog they'd had in their house since France had become occupied and their own German Shepherd dog and her puppies had been confiscated by German soldiers. His sable colouring was different from that of the puppies they'd lost, but seeing him brought back a lot of memories.

Sabine told her all about what had happened and how they'd found Grey.

'You shouldn't have brought him here,' her mother scolded. But Sabine knew she didn't truly mean it. Their mother was well aware that the war had made all three children more independent and grown-up than they would otherwise have been.

'Luc helped us,' Claude added. 'But Sabine crawled out along the branch over the river . . .'

Sabine gave her brother a 'be quiet' look and their mother gave Sabine a 'we'll talk about this later' one.

'We have to keep him hidden,' Sabine said. 'He was wearing a parachute . . .'

Sabine's mother nodded. She removed Grey's collar with its identification tag that bore his name, number and regiment.

'His name's Grey,' she said, and she put the collar and ID tag in a pottery jar on the mantelpiece, so Grey couldn't be identified as a British dog if he were captured by the Germans.

Grey awoke to find himself on some sacking and a blanket in front of a roaring fire. He tried to sit up but a soft voice spoke soothingly, and a gentle hand pushed him back down.

'Rest,' Sabine told him, and he went back to sleep, only to wake again an hour later.

'Get the dog some ragout,' Sabine's mother instructed her, and Sabine hurried to ladle some stew into a bowl.

'Not too much – little and often is better for a dog in his condition,' her mother added. 'And make sure it's cool enough before you give it to him.'

'I know.' Sabine said. She'd never be foolish enough to give a dog hot food which might burn its mouth.

Grey lapped at the unfamiliar-smelling food, found he liked it, and licked the bowl clean. Then he looked up at Sabine for more.

Sabine laughed and stroked his head.

'Maybe some more later,' she said.

The dog would be better in no time at this rate. She squeezed her mother's hand.

'A good appetite is a good sign,' her mother agreed.

Claude came in with more wood for the fire and Sabine told him the good news.

'He's going to be OK,' she said, her eyes shining.

That night they left Grey by the fire to sleep

but later Sabine crept downstairs to lie beside the dog and Claude came to join her.

Although he was exhausted from his night-long ordeal in the river, and his muscles ached from clinging to the branch for so long, Grey was not otherwise injured and once he awoke he tried to stand. He needed to find Nathan but his legs crumpled and he lay back down.

'Shh, hush now,' Sabine told him, as Grey whined.

She stroked him gently and softly sang a lullaby to him and he sank back into sleep, his body twitching as he remembered the jump the night before.

When the cock crowed at sunrise Madame Dubois came down the stairs to find her children fast asleep with the British German Shepherd from the river lying contentedly between them.

His eyes were open and he looked at her.

'You look very comfortable,' she told him. 'Very comfortable indeed.'

Grey's tail slapped up and down once on the stone-tiled floor, as if he were agreeing with her.

Sabine rubbed her eyes as Claude snuggled closer into Grey's soft fur.

'Good morning,' Sabine said sleepily, and the dog licked her face.

They all froze instinctively when there was a thump at the door.

'One moment,' Madame Dubois called. There was no time to hide the dog.

Thinking quickly, Sabine pulled a rug from the back of an armchair and laid it over Grey.

Claude went to the door and opened it as Sabine held her breath.

Outside stood Luc.

'How's the dog?' he asked them.

Sabine lifted the rug and Luc hurried over to the dog he'd helped to save.

Grey's tail flapped slowly up and down as Luc sat down cross-legged on the floor in front of him. Although he'd barely been conscious when they'd found him, Grey recognized the smell of the boy who had cradled him and carried him here. Luc tentatively reached out a hand and softly stroked Grey's fur.

'His name's Grey,' Sabine told him.

Chapter 14

Later that day, Grey had recovered enough for Sabine and Claude to take him on his first tour of what was left of their farm after the last German raid just over a month ago.

The farm's horse and donkey had both been taken and Eva, their one cow, had gone too although none of them had actually seen the Germans take her. The cart their mother and father used for taking produce to market was also missing.

Their pigs had been killed and eaten during the few days that the German soldiers had camped close by. Most of the chickens had also gone and it was a miracle that the cockerel had somehow managed to escape and continued to wake them up each morning by crowing loudly on his perch.

Somehow the goose had got away too. It waddled over as they walked around the cobbled farmyard and it hissed at Grey. The dog was startled, and gave a low growl.

'Leave him, Grey,' Sabine warned as the goose wisely headed off to the duck pond.

It was a hot and humid summer day and the children led Grey out of the farmyard and down a muddy track to a shallow part of the river where they liked to swim and paddle.

'Come and join us,' Claude called to Grey, as he and Sabine splashed about in the water.

But Grey hadn't forgotten his last watery experience. He stayed on the bank and whined. Then suddenly he went deathly still, as he'd been taught to do by Nathan during his infantry training. He looked over to the left where a sound had come from.

Sabine looked too and saw three German soldiers heading down the road. The river was in a dip and they were just able to scramble out on the other side and hide in the bushes before the soldiers arrived. The men stopped in the spot where they'd been playing only moments before.

Sabine and Claude hardly dared to breathe as they watched the soldiers take off their helmets, pull off their boots and socks and paddle into the water.

The children kept perfectly still, hoping that Grey wouldn't give away their hiding place. The soldiers would not be pleased if they thought they'd been spying on them, but they needn't have worried about Grey. He kept perfectly still as the soldiers cooled their feet and then sat on the river bank chatting in German before continuing on their way nearly an hour later.

Sabine and Claude breathed a sigh of relief once they'd gone. That had been much too close. Claude stroked Grey's head.

'I don't want to lose him. His coat is so beautiful, like a grey wolf's,' he said.

'It's called sable,' Sabine said. But she agreed with him that the German soldiers would want the dog if they saw him. Maybe they could disguise him somehow so he looked less like a military dog and more like a farm dog.

'As long as he doesn't look good to the Germans they're not going to want him – are they?' she said, thinking hard.

Claude looked at Grey's beautiful grey – no, sable – and white coat and his proud head. There was something almost regal about him. It wasn't going to be easy to fool the Germans.

'Come on, I've got an idea,' Sabine said.

They hurried back to the farm, where Sabine proceeded to rub mud into Grey's fur, along with bits of old pig manure.

'He'll stink!' Claude protested.

'Good, then no one will want to come near him, will they?' Sabine said.

Claude opened his mouth and then closed it again.

'Good idea,' he muttered.

Next, Sabine took an old matted sheep's fleece from the chicken house, covered it in mud and tied it on Grey with some string.

'It's for his own good,' Sabine told Claude, as the boy held his nose and then started to laugh.

'What is it?' she asked, crossly.

'Now he's really like a wolf in sheep's clothing,' Claude told her.

Madame Dubois stared at the dog in horror when they took him into the kitchen.

'What have you done to him?' she gasped.

The dog hardly looked like himself any more. The fleece bulked him out, making him look misshapen, and he smelt terrible.

'It's his disguise,' Sabine replied.

'A wolf in sheep's clothing,' said Claude.

Madame Dubois nodded. It wouldn't fool anyone on close inspection, of course, but from a distance . . . from a distance it might.

'I need you to take this food out to the old barn at the turnpike,' she said as she put the last of what little she could spare into a basket.

Sabine and Claude nodded. It wasn't the first time they'd taken supplies to soldiers who were trying to help France. They'd also hidden men in the chicken coop and the stable. So far they'd never had to use the rabbit hutch their father had made before he left to take a more active part in the Resistance with the French army.

'Come, Grey,' Sabine said as she took the basket of food from her mother.

Madame Dubois was glad her children had Grey to protect them. Although he hadn't been with them for very long, having a dog around had rekindled all the old feelings she'd had about the ones she'd lost. The children had been so upset when the puppies and their mother had been taken by the German soldiers four years ago and she relished their joy at spending time with a dog again. Plus he added to the authenticity of their disguise. After all, what was so unusual about two children with very large appetites and their smelly, odd-looking dog, going off on a picnic for the day?

Grey sniffed the air as he trotted along after Sabine and Claude. He couldn't detect so much as a faint trace of Nathan's scent as they hurried across the fields to the old barn.

They didn't see any German soldiers as they ran, but when they reached the straw-filled barn and went inside it looked as though the Allied soldiers must have gone too.

'Hello?' said Claude.

'We've brought food,' Sabine announced, into the seemingly empty space.

Grey looked at a particular spot, his head tilted to one side. He put his paw out and rested it on top of a lump in the straw and a British soldier emerged from it, brushing stalks of wheat off his shoulders.

'It's OK,' the soldier said to the other man who was hidden in the barn. 'It's just some children and their foul-smelling dog.'

'He's not smelly,' Sabine said. 'That's his disguise. Underneath he's beautiful and very clean from all the time he spent in the river.'

'Our mother took his collar off in case the Germans caught him and shot him,' Claude added.

The British soldiers looked at each other and shrugged. The children were making very little sense but they were too tired from their mission and sleeping rough in the barn to question them more about their dog.

'Let's see what's in that food basket,' the first soldier said. While Sabine and Claude took out the food they'd brought with them, Grey slipped silently out of the back of the barn.

By the time Sabine, Claude and the soldiers looked round for him, Grey had gone.

His strong sense of smell and the tracking skills he'd been taught led him back to the part of the river where Sabine and Claude had first found him. But Nathan wasn't there. Then he ran on to the place where he'd come down in the parachute drop. But Nathan wasn't there either.

He sniffed at the air in all directions and ran in a large circle as he tried to pick up Nathan's scent. He pawed and sniffed the ground, but Nathan had landed more than five miles away and there was no scent trail of him here.

Grey threw back his head and howled up at the sky. It was the last place he'd seen his friend.

*

Sabine and Claude spent the rest of the day looking for Grey and finally returned to the farmhouse without him at dusk.

'We searched everywhere,' Claude told his mother, defeated.

'He must have gone back to the soldiers,' Sabine said.

They were startled when a moment later Luc burst through the door.

'German soldiers,' he gasped. 'Coming!'

First they'd come to Luc's farm, where the squawking of the guinea fowl had alerted Luc to the fact that there were intruders. As soon as he realized what was happening, he'd dropped the bucket of grain he was about to feed to them and ran as fast as he could through the trees to warn Sabine and Claude to hide Grey. But now he found that Grey had gone.

'We've been looking for him all day,' Sabine said desperately.

At least the German soldiers couldn't take him if he were missing.

'We have no British soldiers hiding here,' Madame Dubois insisted to the German soldiers who pushed their way roughly past her. They'd had a report of British spies in the area, and although most such reports led nowhere, each of them needed to be investigated.

Claude's eyes went to the small pottery jar on the shelf above the fireplace. If the soldiers looked inside it they would find Grey's ID tags and know that although they might not have been helping the British soldiers, they had helped the British soldiers' dog. And that would be enough to get them all into serious trouble.

Sabine saw where Claude's wide eyes were looking and gave the slightest flick of her head to tell him not to keep staring at the jar. Claude tried his best not to, but it was very hard to drag his eyes away. He'd never been so scared before – he felt that he couldn't breathe – he felt he might faint.

Upstairs they could hear the soldiers stomping about, throwing over furniture, tapping on walls to see if there were any hidden panels and opening drawers.

Having found nothing, they came clattering back down the stairs.

'*Monsieur*, look!' Luc said to the first of them.

'What is it?' the soldier demanded.

Luc pointed through the window into the distance. 'I saw someone. He was running . . .'

The soldiers pushed roughly past him and headed off down the road and away from the farm after the person Luc pretended to have seen.

Once the German soldiers had gone, Luc returned home, picked up the grain bucket he'd dropped and fetched more grain for the guinea fowl. Without their early warning there might not have been time to alert Sabine and Claude before the German soldiers arrived.

'*Merci*,' he said as he scattered the grain.

The birds pecked it up and then went back to their lookout wall.

At the Dubois farm Sabine took Grey's collar and ID tags from the pottery jar and threw them in the fire. They were too dangerous to keep.

Chapter 15

Back in England, Nathan found it hard to feel relieved at being home because he was still so worried about Grey. During the three weeks they'd spent apart he'd missed him terribly and often dreamt about him. Sometimes they were happy dreams in which he was reunited with the dog. Sometimes they were sad dreams in which Grey hadn't survived the drop and Nathan found his body. The worst dreams of all were the terrible ones in which Grey needed him. The dog barked and whined for his help but, however hard he tried, Nathan could never reach him in time. From those dreams he woke with tears on his face, only to remember that they weren't real.

'Just a dream,' he told himself. But the harsh reality was that he didn't know where Grey was or what had happened to him.

On the night of the parachute drop he'd dragged the injured French Resistance fighter, Jacques Dubois, back to his motorcycle and managed to drive it with Jacques clinging on behind him, barely conscious, to the emergency rendezvous point on the beach. Once they got there it was decided that it was too dangerous to send the information Jacques had given him over the radio. No one wanted the German army to suspect that they'd been tricked into believing the Allied attack was taking place in one place when it was actually going to be in another. Not while they could still do anything about it and thwart the attack.

Nathan was ordered to sail on a boat back

to England to hand over the information in person.

Once he'd told Major Parry everything he knew, Nathan asked if he could return immediately to France to search for Grey. Major Parry looked grim as he shook his head.

'It's too dangerous,' he told Nathan. 'If you were caught and interrogated our plans would be discovered.'

'But . . .'

'No, soldier,' Major Parry said. 'You'll be returning to France along with hundreds of thousands of Allied soldiers soon enough.'

The other soldiers at the base camp didn't understand that for him, losing Grey was like losing his best friend. They'd spent every single day together since they'd met and losing him left a great empty hole inside him.

Nathan wrote to Penny to tell her that Grey was missing and must be presumed dead. At least she'd understand how he was feeling.

As more days and then a week passed, Nathan fretted that there was no news of Grey. He desperately hoped that if the dog had survived the drop, someone was taking care of him. His only comfort was in knowing that if any dog could survive alone in France it would be Grey. He'd survived as a stray dog on the streets of Dover and British streets weren't so different from French ones.

Grey desperately tried to pick up the scent of Nathan for days and days without any success. He was hungry and lost. The last meal he'd eaten had been a large rat the evening before, so when he spotted something that looked similar to a rat, in that it was about the same size, he pounced.

Grey's head went down and then snapped back up even faster as his sensitive nose encountered the sharpness of the hedgehog's bristles. Grey hopped back in surprise and looked at the creature that had hurt him. He growled at it. Then he went towards it again, intending to bite it, only to find the hedgehog was now curled safely into a ball and first it was Grey's nose that got prickled again, and then his tongue.

Grey barked at the hedgehog as he hopped backwards away from it. Then he reached out his front paw to touch it and ended up giving a yelp and hopping away again as a spine spiked his pad.

Grey barked and barked at the creature that had hurt him, but it remained tightly curled in its ball, safe from the dog's unwanted attention.

Grey lay down and waited for it to uncurl and when it didn't, he eventually gave up and went to the river to cool off. He still wore the last remnants of the disguise Sabine had made for him and flies buzzed around him whenever he stopped moving. He bit at them but all they did was fly away and then come straight back again.

Grey took a long, refreshing drink from the river and dipped the paw that had been pricked into the cool water. It was a hot day and the fleece was heavy on him. He swam out into the water and the last of the fleece disguise finally dislodged itself.

Grey came out of the water smelling much better and shook himself vigorously, leaving the fleece to sink.

His thirst quenched and his body cooled by the water, Grey's hunger still remained.

As night fell, he scratched a bed from the soft forest earth and lay down. His thick fur kept him warm but he didn't sleep. He lay awake with his head on his paws. Somewhere out there was Nathan but he didn't know where, and as often as he sniffed the air he couldn't detect any scent of him.

The clouds shifted and the sky above was

clear. The forest was silent apart from the sounds of night creatures. Finally Grey slept, only to be woken at dawn by the sound of lowing. He opened his eyes and found himself looking right into the soft brown eyes of a brindled brown cow, which was towering above him. She had a white belly and head and eyes that had brown patches over them.

Frightened, he stayed very still as the beast stood over him. And then he was relieved to feel the lick of the cow's massive tongue on his fur.

Eva had run out of the cowshed and into the trees of the Brotonne Forest, terrified when the German soldiers began shooting at her farm.

She'd never lived in a wood before – never lived anywhere other than a farm – but the forest suited her just fine, apart from making her feel a little lonely. The wild boar that lived there were mostly nocturnal and skittered away if she even came close.

Eva led Grey to the clearing where she spent her days and watched as he chased a rabbit, before lowering her head to eat the rich forest grass. Grey chased the rabbit out of the clearing and into the trees before he lost it, only to spot a squirrel, chase after it, but lose that too. He returned to Eva who was now lying on the grass in the sunshine. He went to join her and flopped down but then saw another rabbit. This time he caught it and his hunger was finally satiated as he gulped the rabbit down.

As Grey and Eva spent a lazy time together, Nathan and the Allied forces spent a frenzied day in the final stages of preparation for the mission to liberate France.

'It's on and it's taking place tonight.'

'Right, lads,' said Major Parry in the briefing room. 'The plan is for you paratroopers to land in France first and prepare the way by taking out any major guns and bridges you can before the bulk of the force arrives at dawn.'

'The intention is still to trick the German army into believing the attack will take place elsewhere,' he continued, 'and we'll be dropping thousands of fake dummy men called Ruperts over the Pas-de-Calais area at the same time as the Normandy invasion begins, to try and pull the wool over Hitler's eyes.'

Once the order was given, thousands of Allied aircraft – transport planes, military gliders and bomber planes – filled the sky like a cloud of locusts.

At her grandparents' farm in Kent, Penny was awoken by the insect-like droning sound of the Allied planes on their way to Normandy. As she watched them from her bedroom window she didn't know if Nathan was on one of them or not, but the mission to take back the country for the French people was no longer a secret.

'Be safe Nathan and Grey,' she whispered.

She'd had Nathan's letter telling her Grey was missing and probably dead but she didn't believe it, not for one minute. She was sure Grey was alive and out there somewhere. He had to be because she wanted him to be so badly.

Mrs Green also saw the planes fly overhead from where she stood by Dover Castle.

Dover port was busy with soldiers, some of them acting as decoys. Most would be travelling to Normandy on ships from further along the coast in the morning.

As another wounded pilot was brought up the hill to the castle to be treated in the underground hospital, she longed, as she did every day, for the war to be finally over and for Nathan to come home safely.

It was dark when a faint droning sound woke Grey and Eva as they lay close to each other in the forest. Grey opened his eyes and then sat up at the sight of a family of wild boar, playing in the dark of the night-time.

He'd seen pigs at the Ringway airbase with Nathan, but he'd never seen wild boar before and they smelt different though similar to domesticated pigs. The mother was about as tall as Grey, but much stockier. Her skin was a brown colour and she was covered with tough bristles.

The wild boar piglets that came scampering after her were candy-striped in brown, black and white. They ran around squealing and chasing each other in a puppy-like way while their mother dug into the ground seeking out roots and worms. One piglet rooted up a worm and snuffled it down only to have a second piglet grab hold of his little tail. The first piglet squealed and the two of them were soon chasing after each other, before Eva sat up and they ran back to their mother in fright.

Grey looked up as the droning grew louder.

Little did he know that it was the sound of the Allied planes on their way to free France.

The drone of the aircraft grew ever louder, until the sound was right above them and almost deafening. The frightened wild boar ran back to their nest of vegetation for cover. And Grey ran too, not away from the planes, but in the direction they took, towards the coast, as Eva gave a bellow of goodbye.

The night sky around Nathan's plane was soon lit with orange flames. He could hear the sounds of guns firing. Nathan and the other soldiers were restless. No one wanted to wait. They all knew they could be killed by enemy fire as they parachuted down – but at least they'd have a chance. They'd be doing something instead of waiting inside the plane, which was a far larger target than a single paratrooper would be.

'Let us out!' the men on Nathan's plane shouted to Sergeant Harris.

The static wire along the centre of the plane to which each of them had clipped their parachute clip was needed to operate the parachutes once they reached 600 feet. If they didn't get out before the plane was hit they'd have no chance of survival. There were so many men crammed into the plane that there was barely room for them to move, other than in their appointed positions. They were sitting ducks inside the plane.

'We have to wait for the red light,' Sergeant Harris shouted back. But out of the hatch he could see more and more planes being shot down and he didn't want his men to die without having a chance to survive.

'Equipment check, strap on!' he yelled. There followed a frantic few minutes as the men followed the instructions they'd learned during their training, and leapt out into the night sky.

The plane's right wing was ablaze as the last man jumped and the pilot parachuted out too.

Chapter 16

As Grey raced towards the coastline after the planes he heard the chattering *chi chi chi* sound of alarmed guinea fowl. The day had dawned bright and clear but the drone of the Allied planes continued and it had left them in a state of panic. To Grey the flock of large grey birds looked similar to the chickens he'd seen at the farm in Kent, but not quite the same. He stopped running and went a little closer, only to have first one bird and then all of the birds come at him.

One bird wouldn't have intimidated Grey.

Nor would two or three, but many terrified guinea fowls squawking their alarm cry and charging him was too much and Grey turned and ran on.

Before him was a vast expanse of dunes and sand leading to the sea, and lying among the sand dunes there was a solitary plane. Grey raced towards it over the sand dunes, only to suddenly yelp in pain and stop. He'd stepped on a jagged piece of shrapnel buried in the sand. He felt a wave of agony sweep through him and he bit at his paw to try to remove the iron debris left from an exploded gun shell, but the fragment was embedded too deep and he couldn't remove it.

He tried to run on but it was too painful to even touch the paw to the ground. He hobbled three-legged to the plane. It had lost both its wings as it had come crashing to the ground, and most of its tail. The front of it was also mostly gone, leaving a large entrance hole.

Before it fell the plane had caught fire and Grey could still detect the faint lingering smell of smoke. He sniffed again and crept closer. The pilot of the plane had parachuted from it as soon as it had been hit. Not to have done so would have meant certain death.

Grey peered into the wrecked plane and then went inside, giving a shrill yelp of agony from the pain in his paw as he lay down in his new den.

A day that had started so bright and sunny soon turned cloudy, but the plane kept him dry during the rainstorm that followed and he found the sound of droplets tapping on the plane's metal casing oddly soothing. Grey dozed and then slept.

'What have we here, then?' a voice asked in French.

Grey couldn't understand the actual words but the tone of the man's voice was kind. He looked up at the old man with the wrinkled, weather-beaten face and merry brown eyes, silently begging him to stop the pain he was feeling. 'Looks like you're in a sorry state, dog.'

The old man shook his head as he poured some water from an earthenware jar into his hand and held it close to Grey for him to lap at.

'The name's Elijah,' he told the dog, as he looked at the painful paw Grey was holding up. 'Elijah Buckley and I'd say it's your lucky day – and mine too.' He gestured to the swastika painted on the side of the plane. 'It won't mean anything to you, dog, but this is a German bomber. I feel they owe me a bit of shelter.'

Only a few days before Elijah had had a horse and a caravan, but they'd been confiscated by the German invaders. For the last few nights he'd slept under hedgerows, but tonight he needed somewhere dry. His bones were too old for sleeping rough in the rain.

'Back in a minute,' he told the dog, as he went to collect twigs to make a fire. When he came back, Grey was licking his injured paw. 'It'll get infected if you keep doing that,' Elijah told him. That paw would need seeing to but the dog wasn't going to like it. 'Looks nasty.'

Elijah had lived as a traveller all his life, although he was now without a caravan. His grandmother had taught him the old ways of healing and now he collected the herbs and plants he would need to help Grey to get better.

Then he made some gruel on the fire, added the herbs to it and gave the meal to Grey on a plate. Although he was in a lot of pain, Grey was still hungry and he licked it all up as Elijah made himself a separate bowl of gruel without any herbs.

As Grey ate, his eyelids grew more and more droopy until he could barely keep awake.

'That'll be enough,' Elijah said, at last.

The herbs had done their job.

As Grey lay unconscious on the ground, Elijah cut open the paw and removed the piece of iron shrapnel, sewed Grey's paw up again and put a poultice on it.

Grey slept for the rest of the day but in the evening he heard a sound unlike any he'd ever heard before and his eyes opened wide.

Elijah was playing his fiddle into the night sky and Grey was entranced by the sound.

'You like that, do you?' Elijah asked, noting the dog's interest.

When he stopped playing, Grey made a small whine of disappointment and so Elijah played another tune and another after that, until the sky was completely dark and a full moon looked down on dog and man sitting by the German bomber plane. During the music, Grey would make small sounds, part whine, part howl, as if he were trying to join in.

'I wonder where you've come from,' mused Elijah to himself. 'Shame to see a nice dog like you on your own. Got someone looking for you, eh boy?'

And all the while, only a few miles further along the beach, the Allies and the occupiers fought each other with guns and mortars and grenades and the sky was bright with rockets and flames.

'Time for bed,' Elijah yawned, and he wrapped himself in the pilot's coat, which had been left behind.

Elijah and Grey slept soundly together in the body of the plane as the battle continued to free France.

In the morning, Grey was a little better and he ate some of the fish Elijah had caught while he'd been sleeping the day before. His paw was still very tender so Elijah wrapped seaweed around it and tied it carefully in place.

'No walking for you today, dog,' he said.

Every day for the next week they ate fish, and every evening Elijah played his fiddle and sometimes Grey joined in and sometimes, when the music was sad, his eyes took on a faraway look and he lay still and just listened.

By the time the early morning mist rose over the sea on the seventh day, Grey's paw was healed and he was gone.

As he lit the camp fire to make his breakfast, Elijah grinned as he remembered Grey's 'singing'. He'd miss the dog and wished he could have stayed with him for longer, but a traveller would never stop a fellow traveller from going on his way.

The bomber was not as cosy as his caravan had been, but it would do as a home for now.

Chapter 17

Otto felt much too hot in his German uniform even though he'd taken his boots off while he fished.

'It's all right for you,' he told his German Shepherd guard dog, Wolf. 'You don't have to wear clothes.'

Wolf looked at him and panted. He always preferred the snow to the sun.

'I guess I don't have to wear a fur coat like you,' Otto agreed. 'But if you'd just go in the water you could cool off.'

But Wolf, like more than one German

Shepherd Otto had known, was not very keen on water and would only do so much as dip his paws into it if he could help it. Otto was very familiar with the German Shepherd breed. He admired their courage and intelligence and he had played a part in gathering as many as he could from French farmers to be trained up as German war dogs. Four years ago, he had taken a whole litter of puppies from the Dubois family, not far from here.

Grey caught the scent of fish on the air, and wandered down to the river's edge. As he lowered his head to drink the water, Otto spotted the sable-coated German Shepherd, but he didn't let on that he'd seen him.

A moment later, Wolf spotted him too.

Grey lifted his head from the river to see another German Shepherd dog running towards him, barking aggressively. Wolf was a guard dog who'd been in the army since he was a puppy.

Grey turned to face this strange dog, the hackles along his back rising. But Wolf, who only moments before had been snarling at Grey, suddenly stopped and wagged his tail in the hope of making a new friend. Then dipped his head over his front paws in a play bow. Grey returned the older dog's play bow and the two dogs ran to greet each other and were soon nose to nose as they sniffed their hellos, tails wagging constantly. All their initial hesitancy and fear was forgotten.

Otto strolled over to the dogs, acting as if he wasn't really interested in Grey, but holding out a tantalizing piece of bratwurst sausage nevertheless. He dropped it on the ground close to Grey but not too close.

The smell of the sausage made Grey drool and he swallowed it down in one gulp.

Otto threw more sausage, and some for Wolf as well, but this time he dropped it a little closer to himself, though still without looking at Grey.

Grey ate the second bit of sausage and looked up hopefully for more, but his wariness was still holding him back. However, another chunk of sausage appeared, without any alarming movements from the soldier, so Grey plucked up the courage to approach it and gobble it down.

In no time at all he was sitting with Wolf beside Otto and sharing his picnic. He even let Otto stroke him and didn't realize until it was too late that Otto intended to capture him.

Grey struggled violently against the noose that Otto slipped over his neck, but it was no good; he was well and truly caught and there was no escaping. Otto put him into the jeep and started the engine.

'What have we here?' The kommandant asked when Otto returned to the camp with Grey.

'He's a lost German guard dog,' Otto said, although he didn't know if this was true. But the dog certainly looked as though he could be one and this was the only way he'd be allowed to keep him.

The kommandant nodded. They needed more dogs to protect the railway gun that had arrived and for which they were now responsible.

'No collar on him?'

Otto shook his head.

'What are you going to call him?'

'Max,' Otto said. 'He must be a German dog because he's crazy about bratwurst.'

Otto chained Grey to the kennel next to Wolf's and brought more food for them both. He also found a German collar and lead for Grey.

'Now you look like a proper war dog,' he told Grey, once the collar was on.

Grey tilted his head to one side and looked up as Otto petted him and imagined he could understand his every word.

'What stories you could tell if you could only speak,' he said.

The dog had obviously been trained, but he didn't know where and he hadn't heard of any German dogs going missing. Not that this meant that there weren't any missing dogs. This was war after all, and he knew that situations were often confusing and chaotic.

That night he made sure the dog was tied securely both with a collar and a harness. He didn't want him running off now he'd caught him.

Grey pulled against his chain collar but he couldn't get free because of the additional harness, which wouldn't let him pull his head back. Finally he lay down and Wolf, who wasn't chained up, lay down beside him.

Both dogs were fast asleep but they immediately woke up when an enormous freight train pulled into the camp. It was carrying the massive railway gun from where it had been hidden further along the coast, and the train was the only machine powerful enough to pull it along.

The soldiers were excited to see it arrive, and jokingly dared each other to climb up. The gun was so vast they discovered that twenty-two of them could stand side by side along its barrel. The men who had accompanied it swiftly and skilfully built an igloo-like bunker over the top to try to disguise the gun from the Allies.

'You will guard this gun night and day. With your lives if necessary,' the kommandant shouted to his soldiers. It was a very important long-range firing gun and he was desperate to make sure the Allies didn't take it from them, or even destroy it.

'Alert me immediately if you detect anything out of the ordinary,' he bellowed.

'Yes, sir,' said Otto's colleague, Fritz, saluting and clicking his heels together. He clipped

Wolf's lead to his collar. 'I'll take the first watch,' he told Otto. 'You'll take the second.'

The next morning, Otto took Grey for an early walk along the beach and through the forest on his lead and harness, so they could both stretch their legs before they had to take over from Fritz and Wolf.

But, almost as soon as they got into the trees, Grey caught the smell of a rabbit on the crisp morning air and pulled on his lead. Otto had had a dog called Gretel in his native Bavaria – she'd loved to chase rabbits, and sometimes caught them too. He wanted to trust this dog and let him off the lead but he'd only just caught him and he'd be in trouble from the kommandant if he lost him.

Instead of letting him run free, Otto ran through the trees with Grey still on his lead.

'Watch out for Wolpertingers,' Otto laughed as they loped along together.

Bavarian folklore said that horned rabbits or Wolpertingers lived in large forests. As a little boy he'd been frightened of the stories, but not any more. Now he knew there were many more real things to be frightened of than imaginary ones.

He missed Bavaria more than he could ever have believed possible and he longed for the war to be over so he could go home. But he knew he might not live to see that day.

'The French Resistance have reported that the Germans now have an enormous railway gun in this area. Our aim is to reach it and destroy it before it can do any more harm,' Major Parry told his men, who had all luckily survived the drop and had set up headquarters in a bombed-out, half-demolished, one-roomed school. He spread out the large-scale map on a desk to show them the positions each of them needed to be in. The gun was ten miles to the north of their location.

'Green, you'll come from the rear here . . .' he said, pointing to the spot with the pencil he usually kept behind his ear.

Nathan nodded.

'Timms and George, you move in from this angle,' the major continued as he outlined the plan. 'Solomon and Carter here.'

The men leant forward as he spoke, concentrating hard.

'We'll set off at midnight,' he said finally, when he'd told them all they needed to know. 'Till then try and get some sleep.'

Nathan lay by the classroom wall and thought about Grey as the other soldiers made themselves as comfortable as they could in the school with no roof. He didn't expect to sleep, but was so exhausted that he was dead to the world almost as soon as he closed his eyes. In his dream he and Grey were reunited, but then pulled apart as he was roughly shaken awake. He felt that he'd only been asleep for a minute but hours had gone by and it was time to leave.

'Camouflage up!' the major said.

Nathan and the rest of the men smeared their faces and hands with greenish-brown face paint from the small tins they'd been issued. They left the school just after midnight and trekked silently through the countryside.

It was just after five o'clock when they reached their destination and time for the mission to begin properly. Everyone felt very tense.

Nathan and the other soldiers edged through the trees, creeping ever closer to the well-guarded gun.

'Just ahead,' the major hissed. He indicated to Nathan that he should now head round to the rear of the gun. The weapon was surrounded by barbed wire, which they would need to cut through.

Through his binoculars Nathan could see

patrolling soldiers and a German Shepherd dog inside the barbed-wire fence. It was going to be tough to get past the soldiers, but the deadly railway gun had to be captured or destroyed. It could fire shells up to thirty miles and cause devastation with a single shot, so the British needed to do everything they possibly could to prevent the Germans from using it.

As Otto and Grey headed back to the camp, Nathan crept out on to the beach and carefully circled the barbed-wire fence, looking for a spot at the rear where he wouldn't be seen as he cut through it.

Otto and Grey had almost reached the camp when Grey suddenly stopped in his tracks. He'd caught the scent of Nathan in the air at last and he had to find him.

'Slow down!' Otto shouted as Grey took off, pulling him towards the beach. Then he heard the staccato sound of machine-gun fire. The

British soldiers had been spotted by the camp's defenders and the battle had begun.

As Grey tried to drag Otto towards the beach, a sniper in the watchtower spotted Nathan. He carefully tracked him as he crawled between the sand dunes until he had a clear sight of him. He aimed and fired, then smiled in satisfaction as he realized his shot had reached its target. Then the sniper turned to shoot at the other British soldiers who were heading towards the railway gun from the other direction, but realized there was little he could do – there were far too many of them for him to be able to stop. Meanwhile, Nathan had collapsed in agony from the burning, searing bullet wound in his calf and he crawled on his belly back into the sand dunes where he remained hidden.

By the time Otto had managed to force an unwilling Grey back towards the railway gun the battle for it was almost over.

'Noooooo!' Otto shouted in horror as a gunshot rang out. Everything seemed to happen in horrible slow motion as he watched Wolf leap in front of Fritz and get hit by the bullet, just as Fritz let go of the dog's lead and ran for cover.

Chapter 18

Wolf gave a howl as the bullet hit him. He stumbled and fell, but then started crawling on his belly, painfully and slowly, away from the battle area towards the beach.

On the battlefield it was chaos. The air was full of the sound of guns and shouting and the smells of gunfire and smoke.

The kommandant couldn't bear to let the British capture the railway gun he'd been put in charge of. It was better that no one had it.

'Destroy it!' he shouted, 'Destroy the *Bahngewehr.*'

The German soldiers ran to obey him and blow up the massive weapon as more gunfire burst around them and hand grenades were thrown.

'Retreat, retreat!' the kommandant yelled, as more British soldiers arrived, so the German soldiers ran and Otto ran too, dragging a struggling Grey with him.

As they drove off, Otto looked behind him at the beach Wolf had crawled towards. Wolf had been a good dog and had done his duty but this was war. Hard choices had to be made.

When they regrouped he asked the kommandant if he could drive back and check on Wolf. The officer said he could so long as he was careful not to be seen.

'And if the dog's alive but not fit for duty then shoot him,' the man added.

Otto had expected to find Wolf close to the edge of the beach, not far from where he'd been hit. It had looked as though the dog had been badly injured. Had someone found him? Had he been taken by the British soldiers? He felt an awful sense of dread in the pit of his stomach. What if the British soldiers had shot him?

Grey put his nose down and sniffed at the spot where Wolf had been lying.

'Find him, Max, find Wolf . . .' Otto urged the dog. Grey whined. As well as a strong smell of Wolf there was also the smell of Nathan.

'Find Wolf,' Otto said again, pointing at the place where Wolf had been, and Grey followed the scent trail Wolf had left behind. His smell was strong on the ground and easy to track. As well as Wolf's scent there were spots of his blood. Grey could sense the other dog's pain and fear and he half ran in his eagerness to find him, with Otto close beside him, urging him on.

*

From where he was hidden in the sand dunes, Nathan watched the German soldier and his dog kneeling beside a second dog that was lying on the beach. The dog that was uninjured licked the wounded one as if he were trying to wake it up.

Nathan had bandaged up his calf as well as he could with the first-aid kit he had, but it would need proper treatment as soon as he could get it. Stifling a groan of agony he crawled through the sand dunes with his rifle at the ready.

As he leant over the dog, Otto could see that Wolf was bleeding and badly injured but not dead, definitely not dead.

As he got closer, Nathan thought that the uninjured dog looked very much like Grey. Remarkably so. And as Nathan edged nearer the dog looked directly at him with his distinctive bright blue eyes and wagged his tail so hard that his whole body seemed to be wagging.

Grey whined and tried to go to Nathan, but Otto had a strong hold on his lead.

'*Halten!*'

'Grey?' Nathan said. 'Grey, is it really you?'

Grey whined again.

Otto turned his attention away from Wolf to find himself staring at the barrel of a British soldier's gun, and he reluctantly raised his hands in surrender.

'His name's Max,' Otto told Nathan in halting English. 'My dog . . .' Otto said, looking back at Wolf, 'needs help.'

'You have my dog,' Nathan said, nodding at Grey. 'Release him.'

Otto let go of the lead and Grey ran to Nathan and jumped into his arms as if he were no more than a little puppy. In his enthusiasm he knocked Nathan over and a split second later Otto was the one holding the gun and aiming it at Nathan.

The two men stared at each other, hardly

daring to breathe. Neither of them had ever shot anyone before. Neither of them truly wanted to have to do so now.

Wolf whimpered in pain.

'I have bandages,' Nathan offered. 'I can help him.'

Otto nodded and he and Nathan bandaged Wolf's bullet wound together, united by their desire to help the dog despite being soldiers on opposite sides.

'He is your dog?' Otto asked, nodding at Grey.

'He is indeed,' Nathan told him.

'You could go now,' Otto suggested as he put down the rifle. 'I did not see you.'

'And I did not see you,' Nathan agreed. 'All I saw was a man caring for his dog.'

Otto nodded again. He watched as Nathan and Grey headed off back up the beach. Then he lifted Wolf in his arms and carried him to the jeep, talking softly to him all the time. He felt sorry for the military dogs that were injured or shot or blown up. How were they supposed to know they should hide when a man aimed a rifle at them? All they'd see was a big stick. They might not even realize that what came after the loud bang could hurt or even kill them. How could they know?

Otto recalled the Dubois family and the day he had taken the German Shepherd puppies from their farm. Now it was time for him to return Wolf to them.

'You'll be safe there,' he told him as they drove off.

Grey was over the moon to be back with Nathan and almost danced with joy along the beach beside him. As for Nathan, he could hardly believe that they'd found each other. It was a miracle. A total miracle. He needed to have his leg treated properly but he could wait a little longer for that.

All the time Grey had been gone, Nathan had carried his ball with him and now he took it from his pocket and threw it.

'Fetch, Grey!' he shouted, and Grey raced along the sand after it.

'This is my parachute dog,' Nathan said as the two of them finally reached the British camp, after a slow and painful journey for Nathan who had limped badly all the way.

'Good to have you back with us,' the major told Grey.

He stood with the dog as the medics ran over to clean and bandage Nathan's calf wound. Grey whined when they put Nathan into the ambulance. He didn't want Nathan to go anywhere without him and he tried desperately to get in the ambulance too, memories of the way he'd lost Molly crowding into his mind.

'We can't have a dog in here. It's not hygienic,' one of the medics said.

But the major didn't agree. 'This isn't just a dog,' he told them. 'This is a paradog and he could end up saving all our lives before this war's over.'

'Almost home,' Nathan told Grey, two weeks later, as the seagulls screeched above them and he saw the majestic white cliffs of Dover just ahead.

His right hand rested on the top of Grey's furry head as they stood together on the ship's deck. His left hand held on to the crutch that he'd need to help him walk for a few more weeks yet. Nathan and Grey had been inseparable ever since the day Nathan had been shot and Grey had found him. Grey had even been allowed to sleep in Nathan's tent each night. And Nathan might not have been able to walk far, but he'd still been able to throw a ball for his beloved dog to chase.

On the docks, Penny and Nathan's mum and grandparents stood waiting for them to reach home.

Grey looked up at Nathan and wagged his tail.

Afterword

This book is partially inspired by the moving true story of nineteen-year-old Emile (aka Jack) Corteil and his parachute dog, Glen, who both died on D-Day and are buried together at the Ranville War Cemetery in Normandy, France.

I tried to imagine what might have happened had they not been killed but separated on that fateful day.

However, the fictional Grey is definitely not Glen nor the fictional Nathan, Emile. In fact, I do not know where Glen came from or how he and Emile ended up working together.

I do know that their commanding officer was Major Parry, but the Major Parry in the book, and his actions, are fictional. I wanted to include him because the real Major Parry insisted that Emile and Glen share the same grave as they were so devoted to each other. I think Major Parry must have been a good man and a dog lover as this seems like the kindest and most right thing to do.

In the book no one knows where puppy Grey comes from and during the Second World War, according to the local newspapers, there were an awful lot of stray dogs in Britain, plus 200 French and Belgian messenger dogs that were sent over during the Dunkirk mission, and about whom I haven't been able to find out as much information as I would have liked.

The threat of imprisonment or worse for Sabine, Claude, Luc and Madame Dubois for being part of the French Resistance was also very real. In one French village 600 people were killed in retaliation for the murder of an SS officer.

One of the many ways the French Resistance helped the Allies to free France was by hiding soldiers. One inventive French family even adapted a rabbit hutch so it had a much larger room hidden behind it where soldiers could be hidden.

The German talking-dog school in the book is not fictional. It was called the Tiersprechschule Asra.

Adolf Hitler was very fond of dogs and had two German Shepherds. In the First World War he adopted a Jack Russell terrier from the trenches that he named Little Fox. He was devastated when it was stolen.

German Shepherd dogs became known as Alsatians in the UK during the First World War because of anti-German feeling. The name remained until 1977 when the British Kennel Club allowed the breed to be registered once again as German Shepherd dogs.

The dedication at the front of the book – 'For Gallantry, We Also Serve' – is taken from the PDSA's Dickin medal. Fifty-four medals were awarded to honour the work of animals during the Second World War.

But countless dogs help each other, plus other animals and people, during man-made conflicts, natural disasters and peace-time, every single day. I didn't have to look far to find a host of real-life examples, from all over the world, that were very similar to that of Grey saving Molly in the book.

I've never met a dog that didn't love to play, be it hide-and-seek, find the toy, tug or ball. In fact, one of my dogs, Bella, thinks that a walk without a ball isn't a walk at all. At home her favourite game is taking it in turns to hide one. When it's her turn, she's been known to hide the ball in the bin, toilet, washing machine, saucepan cupboard, old and new suitcases, wellington boots, a wide range of assorted human clothing and beds. She usually gives her hiding place away, though, by staring at where she's hidden it.

My other dog, Traffy, who's recently started coming into schools with me, although not as ball obsessed, has been known to try to catch one in her paws.

Like Nathan in the story, I cannot imagine my life without a dog, or two, in it.

Acknowledgements

As ever I would like to express my huge thanks to the many people who gave their time and shared their knowledge with me while I was writing this book.

The personal stories, both memories of life during the Second World War and animal anecdotes, were invaluable.

When I was much younger, my grandfather, Sergeant William Cloves, enthralled me with stories of his time in the Army Air Corps, for which he received the Military Medal, during the Second World War. He never mentioned parachute dogs, but he was a dog lover and I'm sure he'd have loved Grey.

On the dog side big thanks must go to Julia Surman and her German Shepherds, Jake and Rosie, for letting me delay their walks so I could stroke them and ask endless questions.

I'm also especially grateful to the search-and-rescue service whose volunteers spend many hours practising hiding and finding with their dogs in all weathers – in readiness for when they might need to find someone for real.

The staff at Dover Castle need a special mention as they helped to bring that part of the story to life for me. And Ruth Rose's vivid recollection of seeing the bombers flying overhead on D-Day turned a routine train journey into an unexpectedly interesting research trip.

On the writing side I'd like to thank my editor, Anthea Townsend, whose passion for the character of Grey was unfailing; super sharp-eyed copy-editors Samantha Mackintosh and Beatrix McIntyre; proofreaders Jane Tait and Mary-Jane Wilkins; and my agent, Clare Pearson, for her continued enthusiasm for my stories.

I've also been very fortunate to work with PR and Marketing executives supreme Hannah McMillan and Julia Teece, as well as animal-loving Tineke Mollemans from the Penguin sales team, and the many wonderful booksellers and librarians who've been so encouraging.

They say you can't judge a book by its cover, but I think Sara Chadwick-Holmes's design for this one is just stunning.

Most of all I'd like to thank my husband for his support, his help with the research and his willingness to dogsit, provide delicious meals for a frazzled wife and tell stories of life growing up with German Shepherd dogs.

Thanks also to our two golden retrievers, Traffy and Bella, who I like to think would have been great friends with the exuberant Grey, if he were not a fictional dog.

Finally, I'd like to thank my readers who make it all worthwhile and in particular the boy who asked me if I was writing a book about the Second World War that showed it from more than one side.

I told him I was – and this book is it.

Turn the page for an extract from

The
Great
Escape

by Megan Rix

AVAILABLE NOW

Chapter 1

On a steamy hot Saturday morning in the summer of 1939, a Jack Russell with a patch of tan fur over his left eye and a black spot over his right was digging as though his life depended upon it.

His little white forepaws attacked the soft soil, sending chrysanthemums, stocks and freesias to their deaths. He'd soon dug so deep that the hole was bigger than he was, and all that could be seen were sprays of flying soil and his fiercely wagging tail.

'Look at Buster go,' twelve-year-old Robert Edwards said, leaning on his spade. 'He could win a medal for his digging.'

Robert's best friend, Michael, laughed. 'Bark when you reach Australia!' he told Buster's rear end. He tipped the soil from his shovel on to the fast-growing mound beside them.

Buster's tail wagged as he emerged from the hole triumphant, his muddy treasure gripped firmly in his mouth.

'Oh no, better get that off him!' Robert said, when he realized what Buster had.

'What is it?' Michael asked.

'One of Dad's old slippers – he's been looking for them everywhere.'

'But how did it get down there?'

Buster cocked his head to one side, his right ear up and his left ear down.

'*Someone* must have buried it there. Buster – give!'

But Buster had no intention of giving up his treasure. As Robert moved closer to him Buster danced backwards.

'Buster – Buster – give it to me!'

Robert and Michael raced around the garden after Buster, trying to get the muddy, chewed slipper from him. Buster thought this was a wonderful new game of chase, and almost lost the slipper by barking with excitement as he dodged this way and that.

The game got even better when Robert's nine-year-old sister Lucy, and Rose the collie, came out of the house and started to chase him too.

'Buster, come back . . .'

Rose tried to circle him and cut him off. Until recently she'd been a sheepdog and she was much quicker than Buster, but he managed to evade her by jumping over the ginger-and-white cat, Tiger, who wasn't pleased to be used as a fence and hissed at Buster to tell him so.

Buster was having such a good time. First digging

up the flower bed, now playing chase. It was the perfect day – until Lucy dived on top of him and he was trapped.

'Got you!'

Robert took Dad's old slipper from Buster. 'Sorry, but you can't play with that.'

Buster jumped up at the slipper, trying to get it back. It was his – he'd buried it and he'd dug it up. Robert held the slipper above his head so Buster couldn't get it, although for such a small dog, he could jump pretty high.

Buster went back to his hole and started digging to see if he could find something else interesting. Freshly dug soil was soon flying into the air once again.

'No slacking, you two!' Robert's father, Mr Edwards, told the boys as he came out of the back door. Robert quickly hid the slipper behind him; he didn't want Buster to get into trouble. Michael took it from him, unseen.

Lucy ran back into the kitchen, with Rose close behind her.

'You two should be following Buster's example,' Mr Edwards said to the boys.

At the sound of his name Buster stopped digging for a moment and emerged from his hole. His face was covered in earth and it was clear that he was in his element. Usually he'd have been in huge trouble for digging in the garden, but not today. When

Mr Edwards wasn't looking, Michael dropped the slipper into the small ornamental fishpond near to where Tiger was lying. Tiger rubbed his head against Michael's hand, the bell on his collar tinkling softly, and Michael obligingly stroked him behind his ginger ears before getting back to work.

Tiger had been out on an early-morning prowl of the neighbourhood when the government truck had arrived and the men from it had rung the doorbell of every house along the North London terraced street. Each homeowner had been given six curved sheets of metal, two steel plates and some bolts for fixing it all together.

'There you go.'

'Shouldn't take you more than a few hours.'

'Got hundreds more of these to deliver.'

Four of the workmen helped those who couldn't manage to put up their own Anderson Shelters, but everyone else was expected to dig a large hole in their back garden, deep enough so that only two feet of the six-foot-high bomb shelter could be seen above the ground.

Buster, Robert and Michael had set to work as soon as they'd been given theirs, with Mr Edwards supervising.

'Is the hole big enough yet, Dad?' Robert asked his father. They'd been digging for ages.

Mr Edwards peered at the government instruction leaflet and shook his head. 'It needs to be four foot deep in the soil. And we'll need to dig steps down to the door.'

Tiger surveyed the goings-on through half-closed eyes from his favourite sunspot on the patio. He was content to watch as Buster wore himself out and got covered in mud. It was much too hot a day to do anything as energetic as digging.

In the kitchen, Rose was getting in the way as usual.

'Let me past, Rose,' said Lucy and Robert's mother, Mrs Edwards, turning away from the window.

Rose took a step or two backwards, but she was still in the way. The Edwardses' kitchen was small, but they'd managed to cram a wooden dresser as well as two wooden shelves and a cupboard into it. It didn't have a refrigerator.

'What were you all doing out there?' Mrs Edwards asked Lucy.

Lucy thought it best not to mention that Buster had dug up Dad's old slipper. It was from Dad's favourite pair and Mum had turned the house upside-down searching for it.

'Just playing,' she said.

Lucy began squeezing six lemon halves into a brown earthenware jug while her mother made sugar syrup by adding a cup of water and a cup of sugar to a saucepan and bringing it to the boil on the coal gas stove. Wearing a full-length apron over her button-down dress, Mrs Edwards stirred continuously so as not to scorch the syrup or the pan.

The letterbox rattled and Lucy went to see what it was. Another government leaflet lay on the mat. They seemed to be getting them almost every day now. This one had 'Sand to the Rescue' written in big letters and gave instructions on how to place sandbags so that they shielded the windows, and how to dispose of incendiary bombs using a sand-bucket and scoop.

Lucy put the leaflet on the dresser with the others and went to check on her cakes. She didn't want them to burn, especially not with Michael visiting.

Two hours later Mr Edwards declared, 'That should be enough.'

Robert and Michael stopped digging and admired their work. Buster, however, wasn't ready to stop yet. He wanted them to dig a second, even bigger hole, and he knew exactly where that hole should be. His little paws got busy digging in the new place.

'No, Buster, no more!' Robert said firmly.

Buster stopped and sat down. He watched as Robert, Michael and Mr Edwards assembled the Anderson Shelter from the six corrugated iron sheets and end plates, which they bolted together at the top.

'Right, that's it, easy does it,' Mr Edwards told the boys. The Anderson Shelter was up and in place.

For the first time Tiger became interested. The

shelter looked like a new choice sunspot – especially when the sun glinted on its corrugated iron top. He uncurled himself and sauntered over to it.

'Hello, Tiger. Come to have a look?' Michael asked him. Tiger ignored the question, jumped on to the top of the shelter and curled up on the roof.

Robert and Michael laughed. 'He must be the laziest cat in the world,' Robert said. 'All he does is eat and sleep and then sleep again.'

Tiger's sunbathing was cut short.

'You can't sleep there, Tiger,' Mr Edwards said. 'And we can't have the roof glinting in the sunshine like that. Go on – scat, cat.'

Tiger ran a few feet away and then stopped and watched as Mr Edwards and the boys now shovelled the freshly dug soil pile they'd made back on top of the roof of the bomb shelter, with Buster trying to help by digging at the pile – which wasn't really any help at all.

Mr Edwards wiped his brow as he stopped to look at the instruction leaflet again. 'It says it needs to be covered with at least fifteen inches of soil above the roof,' he told Robert and Michael.

The three of them kept on shovelling until the shelter was completely hidden by the newly dug soil.

Lucy and Mrs Edwards came out, carrying freshly made lemonade and fairy cakes.

'Good, we've earned this,' Robert said when he saw them.

'Those look very appetizing, Lucy love,' Mr Edwards said when Lucy held out the plate of cakes.

'Do you like it?' Lucy asked Michael, as he bit into his cake. Her eyes were shining.

'Delicious,' Michael smiled, and took another bite.

Buster was desperate to taste one of Lucy's cakes too. He looked at her meaningfully, mouth open, tail wagging winningly. When that didn't work he tried sitting down and lifting his paws in the air in a begging position.

Lucy furtively nudged one of the cakes off the plate on to the ground.

'Oops!'

Buster was on it and the cake was gone in one giant gulp. He looked up hopefully for more.

Mr Edwards took a long swig of his lemonade and put his beaker back on the tray. 'So, what do you think?' he asked his wife.

Mrs Edwards's flower garden was ruined. 'It's going to make it very awkward to hang out the weekly washing.'

'In a few weeks' time even I'd have trouble spotting it from the air,' Mr Edwards said. He was a reconnaissance pilot and was used to navigating from landmarks on the ground. 'It'll be covered in weeds and grass and I bet we could even grow flowers or tomato plants on it if we wanted to.'

Lucy grinned. 'But you'd still know we were nearby and wave to us from your plane, wouldn't you, Dad?'

'I would,' smiled Mr Edwards. 'With Alexandra Palace just round the corner, our street is hard to miss. But Jerry flying over with his bombs won't have a clue the Anderson Shelter's down here with you hidden inside it – and that's the main thing.'

Lucy shivered. 'Will there really be another war, Dad?' It was a question everyone was asking.

'I hope not. I really do,' Mr Edwards said, putting his arm round his wife. 'They called the last one the Great War and told us it was the war to end all wars. But now that looks doubtful.'

Michael helped himself to another of Lucy's cakes and smiled at her.

Lucy was beaming as she went back inside, with Rose following her.

As Lucy filled Buster's bowl with fresh water and took it back outside, Rose padded behind her like a shadow. She chose different people, and occasionally Buster or Tiger, to follow on different days. But she chose Lucy most of all. She'd tried to herd Buster and Tiger once or twice, as she used to do with the sheep, but so far this hadn't been very successful, due to Buster and Tiger's lack of cooperation.

'Here, Buster, you must be thirsty too after all that digging,' Lucy said, putting his water bowl down on the patio close to Tiger, who stretched out his legs and flexed his sharp claws. Lucy stroked him and Tiger purred.

Buster lapped at the water with his little pink tongue.

'Buster deserves a bone for all that digging,' Robert said. 'Or at least a biscuit or two.'

Buster looked up at him and wagged his tail.

'Go on then,' Mrs Edwards said.

Robert went inside and came back with Buster's tin of dog biscuits. Buster wagged his tail even more enthusiastically at the sight of the tin, and wolfed down the biscuit Robert gave him. Bones or biscuits – food was food.

'Here, Rose, want a biscuit?' Robert asked her.

Rose accepted one and then went to lie down beside the bench on which Lucy was sitting. She preferred it when everyone was together in the same place; only then could she really settle.

Just a few months ago Rose had been living in Devon and working as a sheepdog. But things had changed when the elderly farmer didn't come out one morning, or the next. Rose waited for the farmer at the back door from dawn to dusk and then went back to the barn where she slept. But the farmer never came.

Some days the farmer's wife brought a plate of food for her. Some days she forgot and Rose went to sleep hungry.

Then the farmer's daughter, Mrs Edwards, came to the farm, dressed in black, and the next day she took Rose back to London with her on the train. Rose never saw the farmer again.

Rose whined and Lucy bent and stroked her head.

'Feeling sad?' she asked her.

Sometimes Rose had a faraway look in her eyes that made Lucy wonder just what Rose was thinking. Did she miss Devon? It must be strange for Rose only having a small garden to run about in when she was used to herding sheep with her grandfather on the moor.

'Do you miss Grandad?'

Rose licked Lucy's hand.

'I miss him too,' Lucy said.

When they all went back indoors, Tiger stayed in the garden. He took a step closer to the Anderson Shelter and then another step and another. Tiger was a very curious sort of cat, and being shooed away had only made him more curious. He ran down the earth steps and peered into the new construction.

Inside it was dark, but felt cool and slightly damp after the heat of the sun.

'Tiger!' Lucy called, coming back out. 'Tiger, where are you?'

Lucy came down the garden and found him.

'There you are. Why didn't you come when I called you?' She picked Tiger up like a baby, with his paws waving in the air, and carried him out of the shelter and back up to the house. It wasn't the most comfortable or dignified way of travelling, but Tiger put up with it because it was Lucy. Ever since Tiger had arrived at the Edwardses' house as a tiny mewling kitten, he and Lucy had had a special bond.

They stopped at the living room where Robert was showing Michael Buster's latest trick.

'Slippers, Buster,' Robert said.

Buster raced to the shoe rack by the front door, found Robert's blue leather slippers and raced back with one of them in his mouth. He dropped the slipper beside Robert.

Robert put his foot in it and said, 'Slippers,' again. Buster raced off and came back with the other one.

Robert gave him a dog biscuit.

Michael grinned. 'He's so smart.'

'He can identify Dad and Mum and Lucy's slippers too,' Robert told Michael. He'd decided not to risk Dad's new slippers with Buster today. 'You're one clever dog, aren't you, Buster?'

Buster wagged his tail like mad and then raced round and round, chasing it.

'Tiger and Rose can do tricks too,' Lucy said, putting Tiger down in an armchair. 'And Rose doesn't need to be bribed with food to do them. Look – down, Rose.'

Rose obediently lay down.

Lucy moved across the room and Rose started to stand up to follow her.

'Stay, Rose.'

Rose lay back down again.

'Good girl.'

'So what tricks can Tiger do?' Michael asked Lucy.

Lucy pulled a strand of wool from her mum's knitting basket and waggled it in front of Tiger like a snake wriggling around the carpet. Tiger jumped off the armchair, stalked the wool and captured it with his paw.

Tail held high, he went over to Robert and then to Michael to allow them the honour of stroking him.

Tiger didn't need tricks to be admired.

Turn the page for an extract from

.The
Victory
Dogs

by Megan Rix

AVAILABLE NOW

Chapter 1

London, 1940

Misty had a bed of her own, by the fire downstairs, but she always chose to lie on Jack's bed. The soft, cream-coated dog with floppy ears yawned and stretched her large pregnant tummy out across the bed and watched as her beloved owner twisted the green woollen tie round his neck and then undid it again with a loud sigh.

Twelve-year-old Amy watched her older brother too.

'Can I help?' she asked him.

But Jack shook his head. He'd have to manage it by himself once he was in the army.

'Why do things like tying ties and shoelaces have to be so tricky?' he said.

Misty gave a soft whine as if she were agreeing with him.

Amy stroked Misty's furry head and began

reciting the rhyme they'd been taught at school to help them remember how to knot their ties:

> '*The hare sees the fox and hops over the log, under the log, around the log once . . . around the log twice . . . and dives into his hole . . . safe and sound.*'

Jack grinned and finally managed to get the tie tied. But no sooner had he done so than Misty started scratching frantically at the brown candlewick bedspread, tearing at it with her paws and biting at it with her teeth.

'Misty, no!' said Jack.

Misty stopped, mid-scratch, and looked over at him, her soft brown eyes staring straight into his.

She'd been acting very oddly over the past few days – crying and hiding in corners and under the kitchen dresser, ripping Jack and Amy's father's newspaper to shreds before he'd even had a chance to read it. She'd already pulled the bedspread off Jack's bed twice and bundled it up on the floor.

Destructive behaviour like this wasn't like Misty at all. Ever since she'd been a puppy she had been a steady, gentle sort of dog.

At first, they'd thought that somehow she knew Jack was going away and this was her way of saying she wanted him to stay. But then they'd realized that Misty was in fact pregnant. Once they knew that, her behaviour seemed perfectly natural – they just had to remind her not to act like that indoors!

'She's trying to make a nest again!' said Amy. 'To find somewhere safe for her puppies to be born.'

'Good girl, Misty,' Jack said. 'You're all right.'

He sat down on the bed beside the dog his mother and father had finally got him, after years of begging, six years ago. A black-and-white photo of Misty was on the cabinet next to his bed all ready for him to pack and take with him.

This was going to be Misty's first litter of puppies and Jack was gutted that he was going to miss it.

'If only I could be here with her,' he said for the hundredth time.

But they both knew he couldn't be. Jack was eighteen and had had his call-up papers to join the army. His orders were to report to the basic training camp first thing in the morning to fulfil his military service duty. After that, he'd be going to the front. There was no way out of it.

'It's Jack who should be all jittery, not you,' Amy told Misty as Jack pulled at the green woollen tie that was half strangling him. 'He's the one going off to war. All you're going to be doing is having pups – and that'll be lovely.'

Misty pressed herself close to Jack and then crawled on to his lap as if she were still a young puppy. He could feel her heart racing. He kissed the top of Misty's furry head. He was going to miss her so badly. She'd slept on his bed every night for the past six years, ever since she'd come to live with them as a ten-week-old puppy. He didn't know how he was going to sleep without her there.

Misty stretched up her neck so Jack could scratch under her chin.

'Promise you'll take good care of her?' he said to Amy.

'I promise,' she said. 'Two walks a day and all the treats I'm allowed to give her. She can sleep in my room if she likes, but I bet she'll keep sleeping in your room as usual, waiting on your bed for you to come home.'

Jack's leaving was probably going to be hardest for Misty. She couldn't be expected to understand where he'd gone or why he had to go. All she'd know was that he'd left her.

'Make sure you give her lots of strokes,' said Jack.

Amy smiled. She knew how much Jack loved Misty and what an important task he was entrusting to her.

'At least a thousand strokes a day,' she said.

Amy couldn't imagine what the house was going to be like without Jack there. But she was sure it would be a sadder, lonelier place without him. He was six years older than her and some big brothers might not have liked their little sister tagging along with them all the time. But Jack wasn't like that. He was the best big brother in the world.

Amy swallowed down the lump in her throat. Now was not the time for crying. She had to be strong for Jack and Misty, and told herself she wasn't the only one having to say goodbye. Amy knew that hundreds of people up and down the country were saying goodbye to the people they loved as more and more men and boys were called up. They too would be frightened and worried about when they'd see each other again.

At first, the war had felt very far away from Amy's world, but no one doubted England was truly at war now. At school they were growing vegetables on the playing field and knitting scarves and socks to keep the soldiers warm. But Amy wished there was something more she could do to help with the war effort. Anything for it to be over with as soon as possible.

'I'm glad she has you,' Jack said as he stroked Misty.

He stood up and pushed his arms into the suit jacket. Then he laced up the shoes he'd polished so hard he could see his reflection in them.

'Ready to show Mum and Dad?' he said. Jack was trying on his dad's suit to wear the next morning – it felt a bit like getting ready for the first day of school.

Misty jumped awkwardly off the bed and followed Jack and Amy as they went down the stairs.

The front door was open and there was a bucket

beside it. Once a week, regular as clockwork, their mother, Mrs Dolan, cleaned the front doorstep until it shone. Most of their neighbours did the same. Mrs Dolan stood up as soon as she saw Jack.

'Oh, son,' she said, her voice breaking at the sight of her boy going off to war in his father's best suit. She clenched her floral apron tightly in her fist to stop herself from welling up. 'Your father will be so proud.'

Doorstep forgotten and cleaning materials abandoned, she led Jack to the front room where his father was waiting. This room had their best furniture and ornaments in it and was reserved for visitors and special occasions. There was a black upright piano in the corner, a floral patterned sofa, two armchairs and a print of a seascape on the wall. Mrs Dolan closed the door so Misty couldn't follow them inside as she was never allowed in the sitting room.

'Here he is, all grown up,' Mrs Dolan said as her unbidden tears turned to sobs. 'And going off to fight.'

'Hush, mother,' Mr Dolan told her, and she sniffed and wiped her tears away on her apron. 'Our boy needs you to be strong.'

Mrs Dolan nodded, not trusting herself to speak. Amy took her mother's hand and squeezed it gently.

Misty stared at the closed sitting-room door for a moment and then padded along the hallway to the open front door and sniffed. There was a lazy late Saturday afternoon feeling in the soft, warm air. She didn't attempt to go out. She'd never been tempted to stray although there'd been opportunities aplenty in the past, but the air with its myriad smells from the street was too interesting not to sniff. Next-door's dog, over-the-road's cat, the three round metal pig bins by the lamp post all made her sensitive nose twitch.

She watched as a boy emptied the scraps from his family's breakfast and Saturday lunch into one of them, waving his hand to ward off the host of bluebottles that buzzed round him.

Every few days the bins were collected and sent to local farms where they were emptied into the pigs' troughs before being returned and quickly filled up again.

Misty stepped out on to the front-garden path and sniffed. But then she heard a strange sound, little more than a hum, like a soft insect drone at first. Too quiet for a human ear to detect, but Misty heard it. It grew louder and louder. Misty hurried to the closed door of the sitting room and whined softly.

Inside the room Amy was the first to hear the distant but steady drone.

'What's that noise?' she asked.

The sound was strangely ominous and her parents looked at each other uneasily.

'What is it?' she repeated, her voice now fearful as the noise grew ever louder.

'Plane engines!' said Jack.

Outside in the hallway Misty whined and scratched at the door more frantically. Then came the sound of the siren, wailing faintly at first, but soon growing louder and louder until it was deafening. In a panic, Misty ran from the hallway, out of the house and down the front path and along the street, on and on, desperate to get away from the dreadful wailing that filled her head, thinking only of protecting her unborn pups.

As the air-raid siren joined the sound of the planes, Mr Dolan grabbed his wife's hand. They'd been warned that there could be bombs at any time, but were not expecting them just before teatime on a warm September afternoon.

'Bombs!' he shouted. 'Out to the shelter, quickly!'

The four of them ran from the sitting room through the kitchen door and out into the back garden, past the outside toilet, to the Anderson shelter at the rear. Mr Dolan pulled away the sacking he'd used to cover the small opening and helped his wife and daughter down the shortened ladder.

'In you go.'

'Misty!' Jack shouted. He turned back to fetch her, but his father grabbed his arm firmly and wouldn't let go when Jack tried to pull away.

'No, son, you can't go back. She'll be fine,' he said and he dragged Jack into the shelter, holding his arm so tightly his fingers pinched into his son's flesh.

'But . . .'

'You stay,' Mr Dolan insisted.

Inside the shelter they huddled together as other sirens joined the first, wailing their terrible warning. Jack and Amy fretted about Misty and longed for the all-clear to sound, but they didn't try to go out before it did. In the distance they could hear people screaming and the sound of the planes, followed by a piercing whistling as they dropped their bombs.

Amy's mum clasped Amy to her as a bomb exploded somewhere in the distance, but still near enough to make the earth shake and their ears ring with its horrible, dreadful, ear-wrenching loudness. Inside the Anderson shelter it was dark, but outside the sun still shone. They all instinctively shielded their heads with their hands as more bombs followed the first; they seemed to be exploding all around them. Shrapnel and debris showered down on the top of the shelter for what felt like hours.

Misty ran through the North London streets like a wild thing, heart racing, with no sense or care as to where she was going, until finally she slowed down and could run no more. She was six years old, the equivalent of middle-aged in human years, and no puppy any more.

She panted with exhaustion as, long after it had first started, the sirens' wailing finally stopped. But the panic around her didn't. People ran this way and that, stumbled and fell, lost shoes and sometimes stopped to pick them up, but more often left them abandoned, not daring to delay.

No one had any time to pay attention to Misty or even notice that she was lost and alone. They were too busy running for safety themselves to hear her whimpering or see her trembling.

Misty wasn't as confident as some dogs. She'd always been more hesitant, reserved, and, although she loved to be stroked, she wouldn't push herself forward unless she was sure of her welcome – even within her own family. So she didn't approach any of the passing strangers.

One woman, wearing a bottle-green scarf, half stopped, but she was pulled away by her friend.

'The very least you'll get is fleas.'

'Poor thing – doesn't look like a stray. I can see its registration disc.'

Misty took a hopeful step towards them and the woman who said she had fleas waved her handbag at her.

'Go on, scat!'

Misty immediately backed off. Head down, she padded on aimlessly, quite lost for the first time in her life. And now she had more than just herself to worry about. There were the puppies that had been growing inside her for the past two months. She could feel them moving. What's more, she knew instinctively that they were almost ready to be born.

Someone ran past her saying, 'Not today, not today, not today,' over and over. London had been warned about the bombings for so long, no one could quite believe it was actually happening now.

'Three hundred planes . . .'

'I heard more . . .'

'Bombs . . .'

'Targeting the South London docks . . .' said the passing voices.

Tentatively Misty approached a passer-by dragging a dog by its lead, but she backed away quickly when the owner yelled at her.

'Get away!'

Soon the sirens' wail started again and more people rushed past Misty. She started to run again too, although her paws ached and she was heavy with the pups. All she really wanted to do was lie down and sleep.

Bright and shiny and sizzling with fun stuff . . .

puffin.co.uk

WEB FUN

UNIQUE and exclusive digital content!
Podcasts, photos, Q&A, Day in the Life of, interviews
and much more, from Eoin Colfer, Cathy Cassidy,
Allan Ahlberg and Meg Rosoff to Lynley Dodd!

WEB NEWS

The **Puffin Blog** is packed with posts and photos from
Puffin HQ and special guest bloggers. You can also sign up
to our monthly newsletter **Puffin Beak Speak**

WEB CHAT

Discover something new EVERY month –
books, competitions and treats galore

WEBBED FEET

(Puffins have funny little feet and
brightly coloured beaks)

Point your mouse our way today!

It all started with a Scarecrow

Puffin is over seventy years old.
Sounds ancient, doesn't it? But Puffin has never been
so lively. We're always on the lookout for the next big
idea, which is how it began all those years ago.

Penguin Books was a big idea from the mind of
a man called Allen Lane, who in 1935 invented
the quality paperback and changed the world.
**And from great Penguins, great Puffins grew,
changing the face of children's books forever.**

The first four Puffin Picture Books were hatched in 1940 and the
first Puffin story book featured a man with broomstick arms called
Worzel Gummidge. In 1967 Kaye Webb, Puffin Editor, started the
Puffin Club, promising to **'make children into readers'**.
She kept that promise and over 200,000 children became devoted
Puffineers through their quarterly instalments of *Puffin Post*.

Many years from now, we hope you'll look back and
remember Puffin with a smile. **No matter what your age
or what you're into, there's a Puffin for everyone.**
The possibilities are endless, but one thing is for sure:
whether it's a picture book or a paperback, a sticker book
or a hardback, **if it's got that little Puffin
on it – it's bound to be good.**